THE END OF NOWHERE

THE END OF NOWHERE

PATRICK DEAREN

FIVE STAR
A part of Gale, a Cengage Company

GALE
A Cengage Company

LIBRARY OF CONGRESS CATALOGING-IN-PUBLICATION DATA

Names: Dearen, Patrick, author.
Title: The end of nowhere / Patrick Dearen.
Description: First edition. | [Waterville] : Five Star, a part of
Gale, a Cengage Company, 2022.
Identifiers: LCCN 2021040903 | ISBN 9781432888541 (hardcover)
Subjects: LCSH: Massacres—Texas—Fiction. | Texas—History—
1846-1950—Fiction. | Texas—Relations—Mexico—Fiction. |
Mexico—Relations—Texas—Fiction. | LCGFT: Historical fiction.
| Novels.
Classification: LCC PS3554.E1752 E53 2022 | DDC 813/.54—dc23
LC record available at https://lccn.loc.gov/2021040903

First Edition. First Printing: April 2022
Find us on Facebook—https://www.facebook.com/FiveStarCengage
Visit our website—http://www.gale.cengage.com/fivestar
Contact Five Star Publishing at FiveStar@cengage.com

Printed in Mexico
Print Number : 2   Print Year : 2022

To Richard and Kitten Arthur

CHAPTER 1

Jack Landon's dressy, white-and-black boots dug one after the other into the cracked earth as his lungs labored like bellows. The gray wool of his summer suit rasped against waist-high weeds that bent and broke beneath his stride. His hand slapped against the mesquite chaparral that alone thrived after the range fire of fire years before, and he adjusted his grip on his writing tablet and forged on.

Through watery beads that dripped from his brow, he found the other men under the shading flat brim of his straw boater. Just ahead rushed two hospital orderlies, their white uniforms dark-stained with sweat between the shoulders. At Jack's side huffed a sheriff's deputy, his face flushed and his fleshy belly showing through his parted shirt. And at the forefront stumbled a craggy-faced man, his silvery hair glistening as he led the party toward the North Concho's fire-bared bank and sunlit waters.

They ran into a furnace of a wind, and it was a desperate race. The aging man prayed and swore, and when he fell to the dirt, he clawed his way up and pushed on under the blazing West Texas sun of August 3, 1917. Burdened by an empty litter, the orderlies struggled too, breathing hard as they plowed through the brittle weeds with the same abandon as the deputy.

Twenty-five-year-old Jack, loosening his necktie as he kept pace, could already picture the impending scene. God help him, he looked forward to it, his thoughts racing in anticipation.

7

Details, take in the details. What I see, hear, taste. Make it come alive with details. And the emotion, don't forget the emotion. Let the reader feel it as if he's here with us.

They burst upon the riverbank, and the images flooded Jack's vision like successive waves rolling in. A husky man of mid-thirties was there, his exposed back burned red, soaking up more sun between his suspenders as he knelt over a supine form. A preteen girl sat a few feet away, her face ashen and eyes glazed. A small boat lolled in the water just offshore, its bow rising and falling with each lapping wave.

The shirtless man was crying, screaming, and Jack came within a few yards and stopped and stared. At the man's feet lay a small boy, no more than eight or nine, but there was something not quite right about him, something telltale about the eyes. They should have registered vision . . . communicated sensory images to the brain . . . done their part to engender thoughts and emotions. But they didn't.

The barebacked man seemed oblivious to their presence, his cries rolling across the bend of the river, and it wasn't until the deputy escorted the man aside that Jack realized how the pieces would fit into the inverted pyramid of his news story. The boat. The fishing gear. The stiff curls of hair dried by the sun. And the waters of a rare, deep pool of a drouth-plagued river that may have claimed a boy's life.

The orderlies immediately undertook resuscitation efforts, and Jack moved about, taking it all in. His pencil sang across the tablet as he glanced and wrote. *Details. Emotion. Catch it all—the blank eyes of the boy . . . the streaming faces of the orderlies . . . the geometric pattern of cracked soil alongside the litter . . . the shadow tracks as the orderly sweeps the boy's skinny arms forward and back, inducing the lungs to expand.*

Suddenly the barebacked man's profanity startled Jack, his

shock and grief finding release in, Jack supposed, the only way possible.

"I'll wring your damned neck! All you care about's gettin' a story—I'll wring your damned neck!"

The odd thing was, it wasn't until Jack turned that he realized the shirtless man was talking to *him*. The discovery was numbing, and all Jack could do was stare into those wide, wild eyes and listen.

"You circle around like a damned buzzard, waitin' for somethin' awful! My boy—he was so *good*, and you wait till now to ever come around! I'll cram that tablet down your damned throat!"

Who's he think he is, talking to me like that? I haven't done anything to him. I'm not the one who let somebody drown. If anybody's to blame, he *is.*

Just as Jack had been at fault the year before.

While Jack was reliving, the barebacked man was acting. So quickly that there wasn't time to retreat, he was on top of Jack, his thick hand viciously yanking the tablet from his hold.

"Hey! There's no need for that!" said the deputy.

The pencil went flying, and the bereaved man drove the tablet straight for Jack's face. Jack dodged, catching the heel of the man's hand in his jaw and neck. Stunned, Jack lost his balance and sank backward.

He must have blacked out for a second, for the next thing he knew, he could feel the baked earth's radiating heat under his shoulder. Looking up, he saw the deputy pin his assailant's arms from behind.

The officer spun to an orderly. "Don't y'all have anything to settle him down?"

The man didn't try to pull free, but he glared down, his puffy face unhinged by grief as he yelled at Jack. "Why couldn't it have been you layin' dead, you bastard!"

And then he spat, right in Jack's face.

Jack lay there, wiping his cheek with the sleeve of his coat as the craggy-faced man who had brought them here ushered the assailant away, the two of them and the girl following after the litter bearing the boy's body. Never had the summer sun seemed so distant and cold. But Jack was no less mindful of the burning pain in his neck and jaw as he retrieved his hat and reached for the tablet at his knee.

Other fingers beat him to it, and a hand stretched toward him. Jack accepted the grip and looked up at the deputy, blazed against the blue of the sky.

"Sorry, Jack," the officer said somberly. "You're gonna have to overlook that. He's just had a rough thing happen to him."

Shaken in more ways than one, Jack came to his feet with the deputy's help. "Yeah," he acknowledged, staring after the receding party. "He did."

Back in the newsroom of the *San Angelo Daily Standard,* a modest frame facility crushed between two-story brick buildings that fronted dusty Chadbourne Street, Jack was filing his notes when the managing editor called him into his office. He was a short, stocky man who constantly puffed a cigar when he wasn't taking a nip next door at the Wylie Hardware Company Saloon. He had the hardened look of a lifelong journalist, from an alcoholic's spider veins in his face to the puffy, bloodshot eyes and ring of graying hair below his bald pate. In so many ways, he was the typical burned-out hack that Jack so feared becoming one of these days.

"Sit down, Jack. Coffee?"

Jack was still too jittery for coffee.

"No thanks." Jack eased into the chair across the cluttered desk from him.

The editor readjusted his cigar. "Say, exceptional story on the drowning."

"You've read it?"

"Made a point of it. Wouldn't be surprised if you didn't win another award off that. Lord Almighty, the things you can do with a story. I've never seen a reporter who could give the reader such a feel for really being there."

Maybe in this instance it was because Jack had understood the drowning from multiple perspectives. For a moment, he escaped the clack of a typewriter from the newsroom and the muted tinkle of a piano in the Wylie tavern and was back in 1916 again, helpless as a flash flood swept his Model T off the road. Finally, he mustered a quiet "Thanks."

"Well, I mean it. I really do. How many awards you up to now since that first one for the range fire? Seven? Eight?"

Jack's ego was too big not to know the exact number. "Nine. Three firsts."

"And that's going against the big papers—Fort Worth, Dallas, San Antonio. Got to be embarrassing, the way somebody from a paper with a circulation of twenty-three hundred keeps cleaning their clocks."

Jack listened in silence.

"When I introduced you to my wife in front of the whole staff by saying, 'Jack's our great writer,' I wasn't lying. Wish I could transfer emotion and life into words like you. And what are you, half my age? You've got a great future ahead of you in the newspaper world, Jack. If I've ever seen a young reporter destined for absolute greatness in this business, it's you."

Jack felt a twinge in his jaw and neck. "You pay a price sometimes to be good."

"Well, you are, no doubt about it. I've been here twenty-three years, and there's been some real writers walk these halls, two or three nationally known novelists, some *New York Times* reporters, a couple of editors with the *Washington Post,* but none of them had the talent you've got."

"If that's so, it's 'cause I work at it harder than anybody else."

"You got a helluva work ethic, all right, son. I just want you to know you're appreciated here." He extended an envelope. "We don't normally give bonuses, but I think you'll be pleased by what's inside."

Jack took it and studied his name written in the editor's florid script. Glancing inside, he saw several green bills.

"Something else," the editor continued. "That new national award named for Joseph Pulitzer. The first ones were presented a few months ago, and they'll be handing out the awards for '17 next spring. I'm mulling over an idea for a series that could get you and this paper nominated. You might even win it, first time around. I mean it. If anybody can single-handedly get the *Standard* that kind of recognition, it's you. With your ranch Spanish, the series has your name written all over it. I'll let you know the details Monday."

Jack was surprised, more so by the editor's efforts to stretch himself—even vicariously—than by the expression of confidence in his abilities. Jack hadn't lacked for arrogance for a long time now. After the perfunctory "thanks" and closing small-talk, he stood to leave. The editor followed him to the door and patted Jack on the shoulder, just like the proud mentor that he fancied himself.

"You know, Jack," he said with an exaggerated smile, "before you're through in the newspaper world, I'll lay odds that the byline *Jack Bedford Landon* is going to be legendary."

CHAPTER 2

Jack drove his 1916 Model T Touring Car out to see Annie that night. They had gone together almost a year now, ever since the start of her senior year in high school. The disparity in worldly experience had never been an issue, but as they stood beside the Ford's running board on her parents' farm, Jack felt strangely distant to her for reasons unrelated to age or achievement.

"You know what we talked about the other night?" she asked, pressing close.

Inexplicably, her perfume didn't intoxicate him tonight, nor did the feel of her head on his shoulder give him the same thrill as before.

"Oh, Annie," Jack said impatiently, "you're just eighteen. Getting married is, well . . ."

When he didn't finish, she withdrew a little, and her chin began to quiver in the light of a full moon. "I just love you, that's all. I want us to be together."

Jack looked beyond her at the sentinel-like mesquites crowding the landscape. Crickets chirped from their shadows, while from the horizon seemed to come a strange summons.

She put her hand on his chest and regained his attention. "Won't you even tell me you love me?"

"What's brought all this on?" Even as he asked, Jack knew full well that he was different tonight, so foreign that he was at a loss to understand who he had become.

13

"Don't you know I just want to make you happy?" she pressed. "We could be together all the time. We'd never have to say goodbye like we do now. We could get us a house in town, paint it white and put a picket fence around it like we talked about. We could buy one right across the street from a school so our children wouldn't have to walk very far. You could work at the paper and we could grow old together right there. We'd be so *happy.*"

"Yeah," said Jack, but the mysterious horizon kept tugging at him.

She pulled away, her chin quaking more. "What's the matter tonight? You seem so far away, like I'm not even here. Is it . . . me talking about getting married?"

Jack put his hand on her shoulder. "I don't know, Annie. I'm not even sure that's what I want."

When he saw the emotion flood her face, he wondered how he could be so insensitive.

"I don't mean *you,*" Jack quickly moved to explain. "I don't mean it's *you* I don't want. It's just that I don't know if I could ever be satisfied with just having a wife, family, the picket fence, and ten-to-seven job the rest of my life."

She turned away, dabbing at her eyes. "I don't understand," she sobbed. "One night you tell me you love me, then you talk like there's not any future for us."

Jack listened to that distant, indefinable call. "I don't know what to think anymore," he said, barely above a whisper. "All of a sudden I feel so empty inside when I think about what's ahead. It's like all my plans, my goals, don't mean anything—my writing, the idea of having a real family again, everything."

She faced him once more, her eyes glistening in the moonlight. "You always told me we'd be together from now on, that you were going to be the best reporter, win the most awards of anybody in the state."

"Yeah," he said lifelessly.

"Did . . . did something happen at work?"

Jack smoothed her flowing tresses. "You always did know me better than anybody." He rubbed the ache between his eyes. "I went over to the river, northwest of town. There was a drowning. I stood there taking notes while the orderlies worked on a boy. They lost him, and his father came up, cussing me out, telling me what a vulture I was, how I hung around waiting for something bad to happen so I could pounce on it for a story. He shoved my notes in my face and knocked me down."

"Darling! Are you all right?" She ran tender fingers along his cheek. "Your jaw! I can feel the knot!"

Jack tried to withdraw, but she hugged him mother-like and continued. "You can't let that bother you! He'd just lost somebody, didn't know what he was saying. If not for that, he'd realize you didn't want to cover something that awful!"

This time, Jack did disengage her arms. "That's just it, Annie. I *did* want to be there. I *did* enjoy covering it, because I knew I'd have a chance to write another award-winner. That man had just lost his son, and all I could think about was another lousy award."

He turned away and kicked the ground in disgust. "That's why what he told me bothered me so, because everything he accused me of was the truth. Even after what happened to my mother, I guess I didn't learn a thing about empathy."

She took his arm. "It was your job to be there, to write the best story you could. Don't be so hard on yourself!"

"I don't know anymore, Annie. Some job *I've* got, getting ahead at some dead boy's expense."

"But you've got such a great career ahead of you—everybody says you do."

"Yeah, everybody says." The crickets chirped loudly for long seconds, but they couldn't drown out that haunting summons.

15

"It's getting late. I'm off tomorrow. Getting up early, heading for Sterling, the ranch."

Jack went to the front of the auto and cranked it to a start. When he returned, Annie tried to wrap him in her arms again, but he slipped from her would-be embrace. Opening the door, he began to step up, and then hesitated long enough to brush her lips with his.

"Don't go yet!" she pleaded over the putt-putt of the motor. "I don't want you to leave this way!"

Nevertheless, Jack climbed in and closed the door. Beside him on the seat was the envelope with his bonus. Guilty, he took it up and passed it to her through the window.

"I don't know what's in here, but buy you something with it."

Unconcerned with the gift, Annie placed caring fingers on his arm.

"You'll call soon as you get back?" she asked insecurely. "Promise me you'll call!"

Jack stared into her features, remembering their past together and considering the future she offered: the white house and picket fence, the children and the school, the ten-to-seven existence of a burned-out hack trapped in a world that suddenly seemed so oppressive, so hopeless, so frighteningly meaningless.

"Bye, Annie."

He drove away into the night, wishing for a light that would show him the way.

Jack didn't go home that night. He took a backcountry lane from Annie's house and drove around for a few hours, and then hit the main road and headed up the North Concho valley. His father managed the eighteen-section family spread twenty miles south of Sterling City, and Jack stopped about four a.m. at the ranch turnoff on the left and tried to sleep slumped against the steering wheel. Vague, haphazard images swirled inside his eyelids, and he eventually sprawled across the seat and tossed uneasily until the coolness of daybreak and the singing of a mockingbird brought him tiredly upright.

Jack's stomach was queasy. His bones ached. When he stretched, his muscles quivered. He felt miserable, and disturbing thoughts added to his unrest. He could still feel Annie's hand on his arm and see the moisture in her eyes. Then another memory jarred him, and he cranked the engine and left the public road behind, determined to follow the dirt lane as far from that river scene as it would take him.

He crossed deserted countryside, passed gray, cedar-dotted hills, skirted mesquite-flanked washes, and all that was left in his wake—all that remained to show that he had passed through—was billowing alkali that quickly dissipated in the brittle grassland.

Somehow it reminded Jack of his life: mere dust blowing in the wind.

The limestone bluff marking a corner of the ranch soon came into view and deluged him with memories. Once, everything had seemed so simple here, uncluttered by the pressure of trying to get ahead in a profession so competitive. Until Jack had turned fourteen, he had been free of the curse that now drove him to write page after relentless page. Until a teacher had suggested that he become a writer, no imp on his shoulder had made him feel guilty for not working harder at a task. There had been no demon like the one now that whispered he could have written his latest front page story better, that he *had* to write the next one better.

No worries or unattained goals had tormented Jack as a young boy, and where was that peace of mind now? Maybe he had accomplished a lot as a reporter, but his achievements suddenly felt empty, unfulfilling, as if his entire life before the two drownings had been wasted on something that didn't really matter.

He turned in at the main gate of the Cross L's and paralleled a brushy draw until he reached the stately house with high gables dwarfed by even taller pecans. Once it had been home, in the fullest sense of the word, a place where a family of three had shared trials and successes with love. But things were different now. Jack's mother was gone, and the only one left was his father, a man who had descended into dissipation after the raging gully had claimed her.

As Jack opened the creaking gate and walked across the grassy lawn, he looked through the pecan grove. Their ranch stretched as far as he could see, all the way to rock-rimmed hills and beyond. Ever since that terrible day fifteen months ago, this land had assumed an importance to his father beyond all perspective, but Jack saw it as nothing but a pile of dirt that demanded obligation for nothing meaningful in return.

Jack found him sitting in the shadows at the kitchen table and sipping from a glass. Through the back screen door came the bellowing of prize Herefords down at the barn, but the aging man seemed focused only on the whiskey bottle at his fingertips.

"Hi, Papa," Jack said.

His father looked up, his eyes more bloodshot than ever. His thin hair was unkempt, and gray stubble masked his flushed face.

"What the . . . I didn't know you was anywhere on the place."

Jack pulled a dusty chair out with a screech and sat opposite the table from him. "Left Angelo last night. Thought I'd get up here early. Hadn't been on the ranch in a while."

"Huh!" His father shook his glass with a clink of ice. "You hadn't been here in a *month*. What the hell you do up there that's so much more important than this ranch? I'd've give

18

anything when I was your age to have all this, and here I gotta hire wetbacks to look after the things you oughta do."

It was much the same lecture he always gave Jack, but today it hurt in a way it never had before. "I've been pretty busy, work and all."

"Work's somethin' you do with your hands, son, like when you got that scar across your knuckles. Not what you do now."

The man took a long, hard drink. When he lowered the glass, liquor dribbled down his chin.

"Hell," he added, "all this is gonna be yours someday. Looks like you'd take more interest in it." He stirred the ice with his finger. "You know the kind of plans I always had for you, runnin' the ranch when I'm too old, breedin' up the herd, keepin' tabs on the cattle market, making sure the oil royalty out of East Texas is on the square. You just gotta be more responsible about it. If you don't know how to handle this stuff now, when I'm here to show you, what the hell you gonna do when I'm gone?"

Jack had learned not to contend with him when liquor loosened his tongue. "Starting kind of early in the day, aren't you, Papa?" Jack asked, nodding to the whiskey bottle.

His father scooted back his chair with a rasp and stood up to drink hard. "Hell, what difference it make? My own son, and he don't even care what happens to this damned ranch."

Jack rose with him. "You know I'm tied up in Angelo most of the time, can't get away to come up."

The older man turned those bloodshot eyes on him. "Like hell! You've never lived up to your responsibilities your whole life. If you'd been responsible, your mother would still be alive."

Seething, he stormed out the screen door, letting it slam behind him. Jack started after him, but suddenly it didn't seem to matter anymore.

With a hard swallow, Jack left.

As the tires kicked up rocks all the way to the main road, he struggled with anger and frustration. His stomach churned. His eyes stung. There were plenty of reasons, even if things hadn't been building for a long time.

The words of a drowned boy's father burned inside like a consuming fire that had threatened to flare ever since the flash flood. No matter where Jack looked, he couldn't escape an editor's smug smile upon outlining a future that any reporter would have coveted. Again, Jack heard Annie's plea for re-assurance that they would marry and have children and live the rest of their lives in the house with the picket fence. Lingering just as powerfully was the stale odor of liquor on a broken shell of a father telling him what his life should be.

When Jack reached the public road, he stopped and listened to the pop and chug of the engine while the bitter dust overtook him. To the right lay Sterling City, and beyond, a career as a living legend, with more awards and recognition than anyone in the state—and maybe a Pulitzer someday. He would have a comfortable life with a nice girl, a picket fence about a trim, white house, and children who would care for him in his latter years. Professionally and personally, he would live a dream, and with it would come financial security as heir to a sprawling ranch.

In one sense, Jack could never hope for more, and he knew it. But in another way, he would have nothing.

He turned in the opposite direction and drove away from it all, speeding faster with every hammer of his heart.

CHAPTER 3

Only thirty yards away, the Rio Grande had risen dramatically.

As the upstream course of the sandy road brought Jack trudging alongside the meandering river for the first time in an hour, he could see the muddy currents through the tall cane, black willows, and paloverde trees that crowded the bank. Sparkling in the fierce Chihuahuan Desert sun of late afternoon, the turbulent waters carried drift that rode the undulating ripples.

With a drouth blighting much of West Texas, Jack hadn't expected to find a rise in the Rio Grande. But at this point he was almost three hundred miles southwest of San Angelo, and dark clouds were rising in the west. Clearly, heavy rains had fallen in the upstream watershed, perhaps in Mexico. That war-torn country was just a stone's throw away across the *río*, whose role as the international boundary was respected by neither the federal forces of Venustiano Carranza nor the revolutionary army of Pancho Villa.

In terms of geography, Jack may have known where he was, all right. But in other ways, he remained as lost as ever.

He had driven his touring car until it had run out of gas, and then he had tramped on aimlessly and hopped a southwest-bound freight on the Kansas City, Mexico and Orient Railway. When shining rails had ceased their push into the reaches of the Big Bend, he had struck out on foot in the direction of the border. Twice, he had accepted rides, the second time from Marfa down through Pinto Canyon. Upon arriving at the Rio

Grande at Ruidosa, he had veered blindly upriver, holding to the Texas side, and now even the U.S. Army outpost at Candelaria was many miles behind him.

But the memories were not.

It was Monday, and Jack knew what would be taking place back at the *Daily Standard.* The carriage bells of manual typewriters were chiming under the onslaught of fingers. The copyeditor was racing through typescripts and marking corrections with editing symbols. Phones were ringing and cigarette smoke was swirling, and all the while the big clock in the newsroom was continuing its relentless tick-tick toward deadline.

They were all there—the reporters and copyeditor and the managing editor, each of them wondering where Jack was, why he hadn't shown up for work, why he hadn't called and wouldn't answer his phone. He could see their faces and hear the rumors as reporters typed *-30-* at the bottom of newly completed stories and rushed the copy to the city desk.

-30-.

It was newspaper jargon for *The End,* and Jack felt as if his life's deadline had already passed and he was living that epitaph this very moment. With his every mechanical step, sand rose up gritty and bitter, irritating his eyes and choking his throat. Or maybe his emotions were at fault, for this was a road to nowhere for a man with nowhere left to go.

The cry came simultaneous with the squeal of a horse.

Jack stopped, checking the Rio Grande at a distance through the riparian growth. He glimpsed only passing driftwood, but when he heard a second yell he bolted for the brush and broke through clawing screwbeans and acacia. Parting the rustling cane at the brink of a *río* out of banks, he heard a third cry of distress and saw two figures struggling in midstream as the unstoppable tide swept them downriver. One was a horse, its head and neck alone visible, while separated from the animal was a bobbing muchacho who flailed desperately. Both of them fought to reach the Texas side, but the boy especially was in dire straits.

Retreating to open ground, Jack sprinted with the flow but found it impossible to keep pace. The turbid floodwaters were carrying the boy away, and there was nothing Jack could do but watch in flashes through the greenery and tall cane. Soon the muchacho disappeared behind the downstream foliage, but Jack ran on and on, giving his all in penance for what had happened in a pitch-black ravine the year before.

Several hundred yards downriver, a patch of white glinting in the sunlight drew him to a flooded tangle of black willow limbs and green-branched paloverdes. Here, where three close-growing willows flared from underwater, a body in a cotton shirt was lodged facedown across a half-submerged limb. Bouncing with the pell-mell rush of the turbid waters, the muchacho showed no signs of life, but Jack wasn't deterred.

Clutching a willow branch on his left, he waded out, contending with a hydraulic force that pushed against his legs and threatened to upend him. Maybe a man with something to live for would have thought twice about risking his neck, but what more fitting way for Jack to die than by drowning?

Fighting two floods separated by time and distance, he managed to reach the boy in waist-deep water and seize him by the collar. But no sooner had Jack freed him from the limb than the surge took Jack's legs out from under him and he went down, buried by waters too powerful to overcome. Still, he held fast to a pliable branch, even as he and his burden twisted in place in the dark currents. For a moment, he thought both of them would drown, but Jack popped up and found footing.

It wasn't easy, pulling a limber form out of a rampaging river, but finally Jack had the boy stretched out supine on solid ground. A young teenager of Mexican heritage, he may have already been dead, for Jack couldn't feel a whisper of breath against the back of his hand. Not only that, but the muchacho was cold to the touch and had a blue cast to his skin. And like the child on the North Concho, he had swelling in the abdomen, as if each of them had swallowed an enormous amount of water in a futile search for air.

Nevertheless, as the orderly had done three days before, Jack quickly knelt behind the victim's head and brought the elbows back until they contacted the ground. Raising the arms skyward, Jack trusted that the action would draw air into the lungs. Next he rocked forward, crossing the arms against the muchacho's chest and pressing hard in an effort to force the lungs to exhale.

It was a five-second procedure that demanded constant repetition. Back on the North Concho, it hadn't worked for a trained professional, and Jack didn't expect it to work here. But after a full minute of induced respiration, the boy began to wheeze and gurgle, and when he began to heave up water, Jack rolled him onto his side and allowed the vomit to pass easier.

Steadying the muchacho with a hand to the shoulder, Jack looked down along the boy's cotton trousers and saw a saddle horse thirty yards upstream. The roan, its wet coat shining in the sun, had safely gained dry ground and stood with its reins dragging.

The muchacho, semiconscious and unresponsive to questions, now coughed relentlessly, and Jack weighed their options. His immediate concern was to retrieve the roan before it wandered away. Starting upriver, Jack could only hope that the animal wasn't as skittish as his father's green-broke broncs, which were almost impossible to approach in the pasture.

The roan was leery enough to require coaxing, but Jack managed to get close enough to slip his fingers inside the bridle's cheekpiece. Taking up the reins, he led the horse back to the muchacho and secured it to a scrub mesquite.

The boy's coughing persisted, but he seemed increasingly alert. He was a stocky youth with light skin and high cheekbones, and there was a suggestion of intelligence in the brown eyes. Placing a hand on the ground, he tried to push himself up, leading Jack to take him under the shoulders and assist. But the boy recoiled from his touch, and Jack withdrew and let him sit up on his own.

"You had a close call," said Jack.

His head bowed, the muchacho only coughed and rubbed his chest as if it ached.

"You breathing okay?" asked Jack.

The boy glanced up, his eyes narrowing, and didn't reply even when Jack repeated the question in Spanish.

Regardless, Jack already knew the answer. The muchacho labored for air, and his cough exacerbated matters.

"You live around here?" Jack asked. "Think you can ride?"

This time, the boy didn't acknowledge with even a glance.

"Listen," added Jack, "let's get you on your horse. If you can stay on, I'll lead him."

The muchacho again refused help, but he managed to struggle to his feet and stumble to the roan. He stood clutching the saddle horn for support, and as Jack came up at his shoulder, it was clear that the teenager didn't have the strength to swing up.

Jack formed a cradle with his interlocked fingers. "Here, step up and you can do the rest on your own."

Clearly, the muchacho was reluctant, but with a strange squint at Jack, he set his worn boot in the cradle and Jack boosted him up. Once in the saddle, the youth sat his horse shakily, his shoulders bent and his chin against his chest.

"I don't want you falling off," said Jack. "You able to do this?"

When the boy raised his head and motioned to the secured reins, Jack freed them from the mesquite and looked upstream and downstream in indecision.

"Which way?"

Still, the muchacho didn't speak, but with another peculiar look at Jack, he motioned upriver toward the building thunderhead.

The year before, Jack had been at the wrong place at the wrong time, and it had cost the life of the person who had nurtured him most. Now, as he struck out upstream leading the roan, he again seemed caught up in circumstances not of his choosing, and he wondered where it would take him.

CHAPTER 4

The Bisley Model Colt revolver with the rusted cylinder set twenty-three-year-old Mary Contreras shuddering.

In this northeast room of her adobe home, she found it alongside .38-.40 cartridges in a cracked chamois pouch, a strange lump under the grass mat as she had bundled Roberto's bedding to wash in the cast-iron pot outside the large glassless window. She feared what the weapon might mean for the fifteen-year-old boy, who had become increasingly rebellious and had begun disappearing with his horse for a full day at a time without explanation.

Ever since Mary had been eight, she had looked after Roberto while their father had toiled away in the fields or as a candelilla wax hauler. Mary had done her best, but now she wondered if she had failed. Regardless, what kind of a tomorrow could there be for her brother in this remote village just above the floodplain on the Texas side of the Rio Grande? Generations ago, someone had named it Esperanza—Hope—but she had come to think of it as a place where hope died with every sunset.

Still, their crumbling, three-room home lay in the *patria chica,* or little fatherland, and it would always be Mary's *querencia,* the home of her heart. Separated by intimidating badlands and the high Candelaria Rim from the Southern Pacific Railroad to the northeast, and by similarly hostile desert and mountains from the populated interior of Chihuahua to the southwest, the *patria chica* was a world unto itself. Except for trade with candelilla buyers and the freighters from railroad towns, someone such as Roberto might have little contact with the outside.

For better or worse, the 140 villagers in Esperanza might live out their years in this enclave of sunbaked adobe buildings, a plaza, and outlying fields irrigated from the river. When not focused on mere survival, they might find spiritual sustenance at the shrines of their respective saints, and in the body and blood of Jesucristo, Christ Jesus, at Our Lady of Peace Catholic Mission under the yucca hill marked by a summit cross on Esperanza's north side.

Until four months ago, Roberto might have been content with such a life, but that had been before bitterness had filled the hollow inside him where his father's love had been. For weeks now, Roberto had spoken openly of his hostility toward whites, even those with no connection to their father's death. For a grieving boy, it was a concerning development that Mary didn't know how to address.

The ongoing Mexican Revolution further complicated matters. From word brought by freighters, raids from Mexico had claimed American lives up and down the river. The entire border was in turmoil, and U.S. Army troops and Texas Rangers were said to look with suspicion on anyone brown-skinned who spoke only Spanish. Mary knew that Esperanza could ill afford to be grouped with foreign elements, so she had started a movement to distinguish the villagers from Carrancistas, Villistas, and Mexican bandits.

For twenty-two years, she had been known as Marita, Little Maria, but the cause was worth giving up this name from her girlhood. Roberto, especially, resisted the idea of making English predominant not only in names but in everyday speech. Nevertheless, Mary—as she now asked to be called—persisted and urged fellow villagers to follow her lead.

It was a drastic measure, but taking pride in things American seemed essential to show where Esperanza's sympathies lay. In her position as teacher of the younger children in the one-room Esperanza school, she had stressed the *patria chica's* connection with the state and nation of which it was a part, but tradition was difficult to overcome, especially for older students so immersed in the culture. With the Glenn Springs raid of 1916, their longtime teacher, who was white, had moved away with his family to a safer environment, leaving Mary unable to instruct students such as Roberto with her limited knowledge. As a consequence, parents had removed the older children and set them to work, thereby denying her a chance to influence them.

Recently, Mary had heard disturbing rumors, and her mouth went dry as she ran her fingers along the Bisley Model's blue-black barrel. Riffraff from both sides of the border were said to be recruiting young villagers to ride with them, and she knew that a troubled boy like Roberto would be a prime candidate. *Santa Maria,* this revolver . . . !

From outside, thunder growled, and through her sandals she could feel a tremor surge up from the packed clay floor. Considering what she had just found, there was something ominous about the way it shook the mud-brick walls. The rumble drew her attention to the open window, and she saw a slumping Roberto approaching on horseback from the east as a stranger led his animal.

Alarmed, Mary replaced the revolver in the pouch as she bolted from the room. In the main living quarters, which were a few inches lower, she slipped the weapon behind a pottery churn on a high shelf above a crude table and turned to the open door. It framed the roan's nodding head, with Roberto hunched over behind and a young white man in mud-caked gray trousers in the foreground.

Not a drop of rain was falling, but the sky groaned again as she ran out past a fiery rock hearth on her left and a lean-to on the right that abutted the exterior wall.

"*¿Qué te pasó, Roberto?*" she asked, unconsciously reverting to her first language.

The boy gave no reply, but the slender stranger made eye contact. Unshaven for a few days and wearing disheveled woolen clothes that couldn't have been more out of place here, he was in his mid-twenties and physically fit, but there was something about his gray eyes that made him look more dead than alive.

"This where he lives?" the stranger asked in Spanish.

Mary noted the accent as she hurried past and reached up for her brother's bent shoulder. "What has happened?" she asked in English.

Suddenly Roberto was off-balance, as if he no longer had the stamina to stay in the saddle, and he began sliding down toward her.

"Roberto!"

She didn't have the strength to catch him, and he would have struck the ground hard if the stranger hadn't come up at her side and helped control his fall. As it was, the boy collapsed at the roan's hoofs, just as a fierce rain began to pit the dusty ground and more thunder rattled the ocotillo thatching of the lean-to roof.

"Better get him inside!"

Even as the stranger spoke the words in English, he slipped his hands under Roberto's shoulders and lifted him to his feet. But her brother was unconscious, clearly unable to walk even with the assistance of both of them. All Mary could do was take the roan by the reins and clear a path as the stranger dragged Roberto to the door. She quickly secured the animal to the lean-to post and followed them inside.

A howling wind heavy with rain chased after her, tossing her simple cotton dress. She closed the sagging door behind her and motioned to the shadowy opening to the right.

"Please, you must step up!"

The stranger navigated the interior doorway with Roberto, and Mary rushed after them across the small room and closed the thatch shutters over the sleeping mat. The rain had already dampened the wadded blankets, but she spread them and helped lay Roberto across. His breathing was rapid and shallow, and he was unresponsive as she positioned a feather pillow under his head and spoke his name.

"River's out of banks," said the young man. "I pulled him out quick as I could."

Surprised at his words, Mary found the stranger in the subdued light. "Why was he in the water?"

"Horse too. Looked like he was crossing over from the Mexican side."

"Cross—?" She turned to her brother, her worry magnified.

Dios mío! What business could Roberto have had across the river, in a week in which sudden rises had turned the stream into a death trap?

Or maybe she didn't want to know.

"I happened by just in time to see him in trouble," the stranger continued. "Wasn't even breathing at first, but I worked on him till he responded."

Mary stroked her brother's stiff hair and watched the laboring of his chest. She wished she could reopen the shutters, for the room's stale, musty odor begged for fresh air.

"I know better than to think there's a doctor here," said the stranger.

Through strands of her flowing black hair, Mary looked at him over her shoulder. He still had a dead man's eyes, but there was also tenderness in his features.

"The first twenty-four hours," he added, "are critical.

Pneumonia can set in."

Turning to Roberto, Mary gently shook his shoulder and called his name, but he showed no reaction.

"Best to let him sleep," said the stranger. "He's got to wake up, but he's got to do it on his own."

With her eyes stinging, Maria faced the young man. "What can I do? He is my brother. I am all he has, and he is all I have."

"I don't know how long he was under, and there's nothing more we could do anyway. Keeping him warm's about all there is. He vomited up a lot of muddy river water, and he probably aspirated some too."

"Aspir—?"

"Inhaled it. Took it in his lungs. All of that's got to work its way out. The good thing is that he was alert enough to lead me here. Couldn't have done that unless he was in his right mind. But . . ."

Mary didn't like the way the stranger shook his head, or the troubled sigh he gave. She began to tremble, not knowing what was to come and fearing the worst. Her father's senseless death had crushed her, but she and Roberto had still had one another. Now, though, a terrible gloom closed in on her, stealing away her tomorrows, for she couldn't imagine going on alone.

The stranger must have seen her shudder. "*Lo siento,* señorita," he said.

Even though Mary had embraced English, she appreciated hearing his words of sympathy in the language of the *patria chica.* Indeed, his decision to address her in such a way made his compassion seem all the greater.

"You are kind," she said. "May Jesucristo bless you for what you have done."

His face took on a quizzical expression, as if her words caused him to search inside himself. Whatever the reason, the crease between his eyebrows persisted as he nodded to her brother.

"If he makes it through tomorrow, he'll probably be all right."

Out of respect for his ministrations, Mary stood. "What is your name, so I may hold it up in prayer?"

"That's not necessary. You can save your prayers for him."

She glanced at her brother. "He is Roberto. I try to get him to use the American 'Robert,' but he is stubborn."

"Stubbornness can keep you alive. It's good he's headstrong."

"I am Mary now—Mary Contreras—but Roberto still calls me Marita."

"Little Mary," he acknowledged. "A lot had to happen for me to come along when I did. I'm Landon. First name's Jack."

"Jesucristo can hear prayers for you and Roberto both, Mister Landon. I will say the rosary for you, and the Mother of God will take my prayers to Him."

His bristly cheek twitched, and he crossed his arms in seeming reluctance. "If it makes you feel better."

The wind outside was howling pitilessly now and banging the loose shutters. As Mary checked her brother's welfare again, she could remember only one other storm so violent. Swooping down out of an uncaring sky four months ago, it had made the blackest night she had ever known even blacker. Only hours before, word had come of their father's death, and as the wind and rain and hail had savaged these same squalid walls, Roberto had wailed his grief at the top of his lungs. Now, as hard rocks began to beat upon the shutters, and the earthen floor quaked to thunder, he fought for enough air merely to stay alive.

Caught between a dark past and an equally gloomy present, Mary could not have felt more helpless, and she found herself turning to this stranger because she had nowhere else to turn. He must have seen the added despair in her face.

"I wish there was more I could do," he said quietly.

"I am grateful, Mister Landon." She found a deep breath. "The old padre says we should not dwell on bad things. We should look to serve."

For a moment, she studied him: the cracked lips and lifeless eyes and the dust that lay across his weary features.

"You are tired and hungry," she added. "Come and I will feed you."

But while the call to service may have begun to calm the storm inside Mary, the one outside the walls raged on.

CHAPTER 5

The wind squealed through the poorly sealed door, but as Jack sat exhausted before a plate of beans and tortillas at a wobbly table that supported a kerosene lamp, he was reliving another day, another storm.

Out of a black sky, a torrent had beat a terrifying cadence on the cloth car top above his head and streaked down through the headlamp beams. Desperate to get help for his mother, who slumped beside him, he searched over the steering wheel for the way ahead, but he drove half-blind, barely able to discern the road. It was the same as driving down a river, the Model T rocking not only to the wind but to the sideways push of moving water.

A clamor began to build, drowning out the chug of the engine. Maybe it was a twister, a monster hiding in the dark, or maybe it was a rampaging gully lying in wait somewhere down the road. One was as powerful and deadly as the other, but rather than heed the warning signs, Jack allowed himself to become lost in words yet unwritten.

How would he describe it all? The crescendo of thunder and drive of the wind . . . the strange, deep rumble like the barreling of an approaching train . . . the violent sway of the Model T to currents from above and currents from below. How could he make a scene such as this spring to life for the reader?

But the greater question soon had become how to make sense of the death of someone he loved.

"You have only taken a few bites."

Jack looked up. The señorita who called herself Mary had brought her own plate over and was seated around the corner of the table from him, the lamplight flickering on the silky black hair that fell past her shoulders. Like most Mexican-Americans he had known, she was mestiza, a person of mixed Indian and European ancestry. Even in his turmoil, a lost man searching for he didn't know what, Jack was drawn to her symmetrical features and shapely form. There was no denying that she was pretty, from the dark lashes and intelligent brown eyes to the smooth and lightly tanned complexion.

"Is the meal not pleasing?" she added.

"Sorry, I don't mean to seem ungrateful. The food's fine. I guess the storm's stirred up some memories."

Her shoulders dropped, and so did her gaze. "The wind like this, with hail and rain." She made eye contact. "Yes, it makes a person remember."

With her brother struggling in the next room, it was no surprise to Jack that her body language showed sadness. His own bearing was probably just as revealing.

"I suppose the sun will come up even when we think it won't," he said.

"Yes," she acknowledged again. "But the day can be darker than the night."

All of Jack's days had turned dark, but he had been so self-absorbed that he hadn't expected anyone to understand. Now he looked more closely at her, noting the drooping mouth and the troubling pinch between her eyebrows, and he felt a strange connection even though they had just met. He continued to stare as she bowed her head in quiet prayer.

"Bless us, our Father, and bless this food we take by Your grace. Give bread to the hungry, and give hunger for You to those who have bread."

With her stiff English, she recited it in rote fashion, but the fervent plea she added for Roberto's healing was heartfelt. Jack wasn't prepared for what she prayed next.

"Bless, too, Mister Landon, this angel of mercy that You sent to watch over my brother."

Jack had not been raised in a Christian home. The only time he had heard the word *God* had been in his father's profanity or in the oaths of ranch hands. Six years as a reporter had only reinforced Jack's agnosticism, for the cynicism inherent in journalism ruled out the need for an old bearded gent in the sky with his index finger stretched out in communion. Neither had there been a place in Jack's narrow world for sympathy or compassion, only ego and ambition. Indeed, he had spent his entire career unconcerned with the plights of interviewees, so long as he could deliver news stories worthy of award consideration.

Jack shook his head, mildly offended by the *senorita's* words. Maybe she saw in him something of which he wasn't aware, but he didn't feel worthy of her appraisal and didn't care to be included in her religion. Still, she had meant well, and after she closed by crossing herself, he moved quickly to make amends for his own breach in propriety.

"I should've waited for you to pray before I started eating," he said.

"It was nothing," she said with a bittersweet smile.

Jack's feet had dried since the rescue in the river, but suddenly they were dry no more.

"*¡Maria purísima!*"

Just as the señorita cried out, Jack found the floor under the table oddly swirling, and when he spun about, he saw water surging in under the door. He scooted back his chair so quickly that it toppled, and then Mary was on her feet too.

"The arroyo!" she exclaimed.

"What do we do? Can we block it at the door?"

But halfway up to the knob, water already squeezed through around the jambs, and the door threatened to give way.

"Take the lamp!" he yelled.

She seized it, but their dishes slid off into the water as Jack dragged the table to the door. He first placed it flush against the scarred facing, but when the door continued to give, he turned the table on edge and lodged it under the knob. He didn't know where Mary had gone, but from her brother's room he heard her frantic summons.

"Quickly!"

Bolting to the interior doorway, Jack stumbled over the step and saw her bent over the muchacho's supine form on the mat. The rising water had just entered the room, and by the light of the lamp on a small table, Jack sloshed to her side with a warning.

"Door might not hold!"

As she tried to rouse the boy, Jack stepped across his legs to the big window and swung back the shutters. The hail had abated, but a fierce rain blew in on Jack's face as he searched the dark outside. Sky fire illuminated the scene for a moment—the wind lashing the lean-to on the right, the horse breaking free from a swaying post, the water churning above the animal's knees.

"Everything's flooded!" he said.

"The arroyo behind us comes out of the mountains. *Los viejos* say people drowned!"

Los viejos, the elderly. In this dire moment, Jack wondered if any of the three of them would live to that stage.

From behind, he heard a crash of wood and a low roar, and he turned to see a deluge break through the doorway.

"It's on us!" he cried.

Before he could reach down for the muchacho, the currents

cut Jack's legs out from under him and drove his shoulder into the wall. The lamp spilled from the table as he went under, but he popped up quickly in the dark with a hand on Roberto's arm.

"My brother!" said Mary.

A flash of lightning showed her down, flailing in the flood.

"I've got him!"

Even as Jack reassured her, it was a struggle to get the boy's head above water and keep it there. But as the seconds passed and the tide filled the room, the currents stabilized, allowing Jack to find solid footing and pull the muchacho up with him. The boy showed signs of reviving, for he was no longer limp, and when his sister spoke again, Jack thought he heard him say her name.

Mary continued to call through the dark, and Jack found her arm and posed a critical question.

"How high can it get?"

"Many houses washed away. Mother of God, what can we do?"

Jack didn't know, and he turned again to the chest-high window. When he saw floodwaters spilling in, he realized they had only one option.

"The roof—can you climb up from the window?"

"But Roberto!"

"I'll take care of your brother. You need to climb!"

He felt her brush past, and against the flare of lightning, he watched her silhouette gain a perch in the window and hold to a swinging shutter. It was a precarious spot, and her ankle divided the pouring waters as she twisted a sandaled foot against the sill. He lost sight of the señorita between lightning flashes, but he stretched out a supporting hand and found her foot digging for a hold halfway up the window frame. He gave her sandal a final boost, and the next sky fire showed an empty window.

The waters in the room were rising quickly, and Jack turned to the muchacho.

"We've got to climb out. You understand me, Roberto? We're climbing out."

Jack repeated it in Spanish, trying to project calm and inspire confidence, but as he struggled up to a sitting position in the window and hauled the stirring boy up after him, he couldn't forget his failure in another flood. There had been no shutter to cling to that night, but as he and the muchacho denied the incoming waters full access through the window, this surge seemed almost as strong.

"Get your feet under you!" Jack urged.

Inside his arm, the muchacho began to rise with him, and Jack yielded his grip on the shutter and leaned out to search for a hold above. When he turned his face skyward, the deluge pouring off the roof half-drowned him. For a moment, all kinds of doubt assailed him, and then something seized his wrist and guided his hand to a projecting roof pole.

Mary was there, hidden in the dark sky, her pleas for her brother muffled by thunder. Now that Jack had a handhold, he hoisted Roberto by the waist and begged him to reach for the overhang. Jack was still unsure, but the world lighted up for an instant and he saw the boy with an overhead grip. It took the efforts of all three—Roberto straining, Jack lifting, Mary dragging—but somehow the muchacho made it onto the roof.

To a long peal of thunder, Jack scrambled up after him and sprawled out in the wind and rain and in the water that rolled down the slope.

These walls have got to hold, he said silently.

But hope and a wish wouldn't make it come true. Nor would they be any more effective in keeping a violent gale from blowing them off into the inky depths.

"Stay low!" Jack warned.

When he had approached the house with Roberto in early evening, he had noted that the roof was not flat like those of some adobes. It had presented a slight slope up to a ridge, and the ribs of its ocotillo thatching had stood out distinctly from the overlay of sun-hardened clay. Now, belly down, Jack clung to one of the long, narrow spines as the gusts toyed with him, picking up his leg and dropping it. Someone was stretched out beside him, and whether it was a Mexican boy or a señorita with whom no stranger had a right to become unduly personal, Jack threw an arm across and pinned the shoulders.

"Hold to each other!" he said.

Indeed, with the bulk of two people, they were safer together than apart, and if the second person linked to the third, the three of them might be able to survive the winds.

Jack hung on grimly as lightning showed that he lay face-to-face with Mary. He could hear her prayers, but he was more conscious of her whipping tresses and her warmth in the chilling rain. He wondered what Annie would think if she could see him now, alighted in another world where there were no white houses with picket fences, only this crude adobe lashed by floodwaters. How would she react to him embracing this señorita, whose maturity and intelligence were so immediately apparent that Annie seemed only a sheltered schoolgirl by comparison?

Jack pondered these things, and more, until the wind stopped and the lightning-rent clouds began to recede. Now it seemed awkward to have his arm around this young woman, and he removed it and sat up in a light drizzle. But the danger was still too great to bother with embarrassment. He could hear the rushing waters below, and feel the rumble through the roof as the currents surged against the walls. How much more could they withstand, and what could any of them do about it except wait and accept whatever would come?

Well, for the señorita, there was prayer.

"My Father, My Father," she implored. "Please help us!"

But even the sincerest prayer couldn't help when there was no one to respond, and the vanity of Mary's petition bothered Jack when so many people were in need right now. Indeed, across the night, he could hear voices—shrieks and wails and names desperately shouted. For once, Jack didn't assess the situation with the callousness of a journalist, but instead with an empathy that would have surprised him only days ago.

The cries obviously touched Mary as well. "What can we do for them?"

"Not any more than they can for us." He tried to peer past her as she sat up. "Your brother's there, isn't he? He all right?"

Turning away, the señorita spoke her brother's name and asked about his well-being, but the boy only moaned.

"He is so cold," she said. "Sh—How do you say? Shivering?"

"He's suffering from exposure. Get on the other side and hold him. I'll scoot in close. We've got to get him warm."

Even after the señorita hugged the boy against her breast and Jack pressed near, Roberto continued to shake. Jack had never known anyone to tremble so violently, but eventually the boy's shiver diminished and then died away.

But the cries in the night did not.

From out of a murmur of voices to the north, a forlorn mother called incessantly for her *niño*. From the west rose up multiple pleas of *socorro! socorro!*, but there must have been no one to offer the help for which they begged. From east and south came other voices, pitiful and pleading as they carried across the relentless floodwaters.

Jack heard them all—the hombres and señoras, the *niños* and *niñas*—a people shaken and desperate in the face of events out of their control.

The stars came out, pinpricks of light sparkling against a dark veil. Soon afterward, a glow appeared in the east, and against it the outlines of distant crags took shape. When the three-quarter moon showed itself, it threw a soft glow across the señorita and her brother. There was something tranquil about their lifesaving embrace, but as Jack stood and slowly turned, the scene all around was far from idyllic.

He saw island adobes in a sea of swirling waters, and on roofs near and far, dark figures huddling lost and helpless. Many of them prayed, their quivering voices rolling across the turbulent currents, while at Jack's side Mary resumed her own appeal to a supposed higher power.

Distressed by so many things, Jack couldn't keep his feelings to himself.

"We're on our own here."

Her prayer interrupted, Mary responded. "What, Mister Landon?"

"There's just us, all those people. Nobody else is going to help us."

"There is God. He will not forsake us."

Jack swept his arm across the scene to the east. "Everything's flooded. A woman's crying for her baby. People are calling for help. If that's not forsaken, I don't know what is."

But Mary wasn't persuaded. "All things are for the good of His people. Even what we think is bad."

That makes no sense at all, he started to say, and then he thought better of it. At a time like this, there was no reason to ridicule her faith. At least she had something to give her hope, while he had nothing but one dark moment after another.

CHAPTER 6

The moon crawled across the sky.

It was the longest night Jack had ever known, except, perhaps, for the terrible hours after another storm had raged. Helpless to do anything but watch by moon glow as Mary tended her brother, Jack could only wait, not knowing how much more the walls below could withstand. Ultimately, though, the crashing waters began to recede, and by daybreak the flood was gone.

In its wake was devastation.

The debris took many forms—driftwood and mud deposits, farming implements and building materials, household goods and burlap bags stripped of corn. Sheds were in ruin, and so were a couple of nearby houses. Worst was the death: the rats and chickens, the pigs and cattle, the dogs and cats.

But all of it paled in comparison to the sound of a despondent mother still calling for her child.

Jack turned and addressed Mary, who sat caressing her brother's cheek with the back of her fingers.

"Any place we can take him? Sun's coming up. It'll be blazing hot here."

She looked up, and then her gaze went past Jack and she pointed north to the village's outskirts. "The mission. People will gather there."

Indeed, a bell was tolling, and past rooftops with stirring figures, Jack saw white-plastered walls topped by a bell tower and a cross, all set against a sizable hill studded with yucca. The church clearly was on higher ground, and people were already dropping from the roofs and bearing toward it.

"My brother sleeps again," said Mary. "We will have to carry him."

"Just help me get him down. I can take him from there."

It wasn't easy, but soon they were down in the debris and slogging through the mud. Roberto was hefty for someone as bone-weary as Jack, and when Mary saw him struggling, she asked a passing villager to help. The muddy man seemed too shaken to speak, but he took the muchacho's legs and he and Jack negotiated the debris through the village. Beyond a plaza and well, they went through a stone arch into a low-walled courtyard marked by graves and crosses and reached the open mission doors under the yucca hill.

When Jack stepped across the threshold with his burden, it struck him that this was the first time he had ever been inside a church. With the same arrogance that had ruled him in a newsroom, he had always felt superior to religious people, who seemed to need a crutch to get through life. Better, he thought, to face the brutal reality that everyone was just a comic figure, careening from cradle to grave, than to live a lie.

Nevertheless, he admired how the believers who flocked to this shadowy, clay-floor sanctuary ministered to one another.

A shrunken old padre in flowing vestments met them, and his crow's-feet deepened as he questioned Mary about Roberto's condition. His assessment completed, the padre directed them down between crude benches toward a looming crucifix that showed suffering in Christ's likeness. As they neared the altar, a muchacho of twelve or so directed them toward a bench before the votive candles flickering on the right. When Jack asked for water for Roberto, the young muchacho called to someone, and shortly after Jack and the muddy villager laid Roberto on the wobbly seat, a tired-eyed señora arrived with a narrow-necked jug and matching pottery cups.

Mary accepted the items with a bittersweet smile, and as she trickled water between her brother's lips, Jack looked back across the filling sanctuary at the growing brightness through the doors.

"Something I've got to do," he said, starting away.

"Mister Landon?" said Mary. "You are coming back?"

Strangely, it reminded Jack of Annie's plea as he had driven away into a night with so many unknowns. Did he have any more justification to return to this señorita than he'd had with Annie?

He didn't know the answer, and so he said nothing at all. Moments later, he broke into sunshine that seemed as gloomy as it was bright.

There was a reason. Across the graveyard and beyond the adobes to his right, Jack could hear the heartbroken mother still calling for a child who wasn't there. In an instant, Jack was back in another time, another place, and it was his own voice that called through a morning so sunny and yet so dark.

Ma! Ma!

Again and again he shouted, a continuation of his cries throughout a long night, but even as he scouted a muddy ravine to which a flash flood had laid waste, there had been no one to answer.

Now, on this August morning in 1917, the mournful summons of a despairing mother led him through a flood-ravaged village far away. His long shadow preceded him, effortlessly navigating the debris that scraped his legs and the mud that grasped at his boots. He passed the carcasses of drowned burros and goats, skirted mounds of melted adobe, waded through low areas where he could look through open doors and see household items floating inside homes still inundated.

Against the exposed adobe of a wall partly stripped of plaster,

Jack found her sitting, a distraught figure with mud in her long, black hair. Her chin quaked and her face was ashen, and her forehead carried lines that no señora of early thirties should have. There was a glassy look in her eyes, and yet her voice was very much engaged as she kept up her poignant cry for a child who didn't answer.

All the while, she rocked back and forth, clutching a *cobijita* to her breast, and Jack immediately understood what that empty baby blanket meant.

"Señora, what can I do to help you?" he asked in Spanish.

She looked up, and when he saw his shadow darken her face, he moved to the side to avoid creating unwelcome symbolism. Would he ever be able to stop thinking like a writer?

"*Mi niño . . . Mi niño . . .*" The words trembled on her lips.

"Where did you see him last?"

"*Aquí.*" She peered down at the blanket and opened it almost tenderly, as if her child were still inside. "*¡Aquí! Mi niño, aquí!*"

Maybe Jack had been a hard-nosed reporter, but it would have taken someone with a heart of stone not to be moved by a grieving mother whose child had been swept right out of her arms.

He reached for her hand. "Señora, can you make it to the mission? They're gathering there, and they'll take care of you."

"*¿Mi niño?*" she asked with pleading eyes.

"I'm going to look for him. Here, let me help you up."

"*¿Mi niño?*"

"I'll do everything I can to find him. *Por favor,* take my hand."

Sobbing, she gained her feet and started away on her own, a broken woman bearing toward the mission. He watched until she disappeared in the maze of adobes, and then he turned and moved with the course of the recent floodwaters. Thirty yards to his right, he could see the banks of the winding arroyo, its flow reduced to a trickle now. As he tramped through the mud, he paid special attention to the ruins of sheds and adobe corrals, to scrub mesquites and gnarly Spanish daggers, to driftwood and other debris—to anything against which a child may have lodged. He wanted to find the señora's infant son, but at the same time, he almost hoped that he didn't, because there was no chance that the *niño* could have survived. Presenting a dead child to his mother was a scene of which Jack wanted no part, but he had made a promise to do his best and he would fulfill it.

Exhaustion and dehydration slowed his gait, but he kept up the search on past the lower outskirts of a village whose name he didn't even know. Tragedy showed itself wherever he looked, particularly in the half-buried crucifixes and damaged shrines of a people whose faith had failed them. Evidence of shattered lives persisted on into the miry floodplain, where he found jutting footwear and shards of pottery, and tattered garments that clung to screwbean chaparral bent by fierce currents. From the fork of a scrub mesquite stared a broken-armed doll, and Jack wondered if those button eyes could see all the things that troubled him.

It was inexplicable that mere water could have wreaked so much drama in his life, and yet the facts were indisputable. Jack didn't believe in hell, at least not one of fire and brimstone, but there was no doubt that he had found his own perdition in another form.

No matter its manifestation, he wanted out. He wanted to escape these reminders of the very things he had fled. Nearing the river with its black willows and tall cane, Jack turned upstream, determined to leave Mary and her brother and the despondent señora behind, just as he had done with his editor and father and Annie.

He managed only a dozen steps before he froze, stunned by what he found shrouded by the wet sand at his boots.

A dead baby.

Shuddering, Jack knelt and extricated the body. The hair was dark like the señora's, and when he wiped the mud from the face, white foam flecked with blood appeared in the mouth and nose. For an instant, Jack thought the infant might still be alive, but the cold, rigid feel of the body told him the hard truth. Too, the sodden skin was white and wrinkled, as if the child had spent a long time immersed, and there were abrasions on the forehead and all along the legs.

Jack could only imagine the baby's last moments as the wicked currents had tossed him about in the floating debris. Jack didn't want to dwell on it, because it made him also dwell on his mother's last moments, and those of the child in the North Concho.

As much as he resisted, he knew what he had to do. But first he took the infant's body through the tall, rustling cane to the river, which no longer was in flood, and washed away the mud. The mother didn't need the added strain of carrying with her an image of her baby so desecrated.

Jack plodded back through the village with dread, mentally writing the story that he was about to live. More people were in the streets now, haggard men and women salvaging what they could from the muck, and as he went by with his burden, they paused respectfully and crossed themselves. A youth rushed ahead to the mission, and by the time Jack passed under the courtyard arch, the padre came out of the double doors. Already stooped from age, the priest seemed to wither more as he waited with sad eyes.

"His mother," said Jack as he approached.

With fingers knotted by arthritis, the padre made the sign of the cross and motioned him inside.

Jack found her down at the front, sitting on a left-side bench as she clenched the blanket to her breast and prayed upward toward the looming crucifix. The depiction of Christ's crucifixion was striking, the blood depicted in bright red under the heart and on the impaled hands and feet. Even as the thorn-pierced head hung to the side, the eyes were open and seemed to stare down at Jack, and they added to his disquiet as he stopped alongside the mother's bent shoulders.

"Lo siento," he said quietly. "I'm sorry, señora."

She looked around and saw, and as the distress in her face became agony, her cry reverberated through the sanctuary. For a moment, she and Jack seemed the only people in the world, and she stretched out her arms and he passed the dead child into her care.

He backed away, not knowing what to do except bow his head and allow her the privacy she needed. Turning, he found Mary before him. There was something in her eyes he couldn't identify, perhaps respect or even admiration, and it comforted Jack in a way he also couldn't understand.

He followed her with his gaze as she sat next to the señora and placed an arm around her, consoling as best she could. Soon the padre appeared, bearing bunched grama grass with which he sprinkled holy water on the grieving mother while pronouncing a blessing. To Jack's surprise, the priest proceeded to sprinkle Jack as well, much of it catching his face. Jack didn't know everything the act signified for believers—grace for body and soul, he supposed—but it was good that, for once at least, water supposedly facilitated something beneficial rather than harmful.

He retreated to the nearby bench where Roberto rested comfortably under a woolen blanket someone had provided. For Mary's sake, Jack hoped her brother recovered, for the observant reporter in him was struck by her compassion for the señora, just as in retrospect he marveled at her composure in the flood. If it was true that a dramatic moment best revealed a person's character, this young woman had already proven herself special.

Just as Jack slumped exhausted beside Roberto, a muchacho approached with water, and soon afterward a rebosa-cloaked woman brought frijoles wrapped in tortillas. Jack was still eating when Mary came up before him.

"How is she?" he asked, checking the far bench.

"The Señora Ramos will not give up her baby."

Assuredly, the blanket had taken on bulk now, and the señora held it to her breast as though the child were still alive.

"Maybe I shouldn't have gone looking," said Jack.

"So that is why you left," Mary acknowledged, as if in answer to her own question. "To find the missing baby for his mother."

"Maybe it would've been easier if I hadn't brought him back."

"It is better this way. Now she can mourn, and begin to accept, just as when her husband died."

Accept.

Even fifteen months after his mother's body had been recovered from the gully, Jack still carried the burden of his role in her death. His introspection would have lingered if not for Mary's voice.

"Of all in the village, you, a stranger, answered Señora Ramos's needs. You are very caring, Mister Landon. You have a servant's heart."

Kind. Caring. An angel of mercy. In their brief time together, this señorita had characterized him by all three terms. During his years of cynicism and indifference to others, Jack would never have believed it. Honesty, though, had always been important to him, and it seemed even more so as he looked into her trusting eyes.

"I'm not who you think I am," he said.

Mary squinted a little, clearly uncertain.

"I've got a long way to go," Jack added. "I don't expect I'll ever get there."

"Where is that?"

"To the place where I'd deserve what you've said about me."

"God gives grace to the humble," said Mary. "There is a Mexican proverb that says, 'Show me the actions of a man, and I will see the man.' "

There had been a time—moments ago, really—when Jack's conscience would have been immune to anything this señorita might say. But now, strangely, he was bothered by how disappointed in him she would be if she had known the circumstances under which he had recovered the body.

Mary edged past him and knelt at Roberto's side. Her long hair brushed the boy's shoulder as she pressed a hand to the woolen blanket and gauged the rise and fall of his chest. From brother to Señora Ramos and back to her brother she had gone, ministering to both after enduring so much during the flood, and Jack remembered what one of his father's Mexican laborers had said.

A home doesn't rest upon the ground, but upon a woman.

CHAPTER 7

Jack stayed nearby as Roberto rallied during the morning, his labored breaths stabilizing. Too, Mary reported an encouraging warmth as she took her brother's hand, and the blue cast that his skin had presented the evening before had gone away. The boy coughed a lot, but it was no longer the gurgling cough that had been all too suggestive of pneumonia. By midday, Roberto was alert enough for Mary to spoon menudo broth between his lips, and then he lapsed into sleep again.

"It's good your brother's sleeping so much," said Jack. He sat on the far end of the bench from Mary, their legs on opposite sides, and studied Roberto supine between them. Mary kept her face toward the sanctuary crucifix, a focal point for her whispered prayers, while Jack had spent much of the morning staring at the mission doors and wondering what awaited him beyond the village.

"He's getting better by the hour," Jack added.

Mary turned with a smile. "It is Our Lady. She has taken my prayers to Jesucristo."

Whatever the reason, there was no questioning Roberto's improvement.

"He's going to pull through," said Jack. Suddenly a thought concerned him, and he searched the señorita's features. "What about you, though?"

"What do you mean?"

53

"Your house flooded. All the low-lying houses did. Where can you go?"

"Home, Mister Landon. I will clean it out, and Roberto and I will go back."

"You can't. That's the second time it's happened, you told me. The two of you barely got out with your lives. It'll flood again."

"In Esperanza—this village—we accept that when God wills, even the saints can do nothing."

Jack looked down, and an idea began to germinate. But if the saints themselves were powerless in her fatalistic world, what influence could a mere stranger have?

Still, he had to try.

"Say I came to you with a suggestion," he said, finding her eyes. "Would you listen?"

"God sent you to watch over my brother. I must listen."

"Would the other villagers listen?"

"I would stand up for you. Already, they speak of what you did for the señora."

"You have the men's respect, and not just the women's?" Jack pressed.

"I am not to speak to them of village matters, but I can speak of you. I teach their children."

"You're a teacher?" he repeated in surprise. At first sight outside the adobe house, Jack had taken Mary for an uneducated mestiza, consigned to a life of squalor in a half acre of hell.

"I have the young children," she replied. "There's no one to teach the others. When the boys are older, they work the fields, and when there is no need to tend the crops, they are left to find trouble."

Clearly, Jack had been as wrong about this señorita as she was about him.

"Would you be able to get the villagers together?" he asked.

"Here, maybe? As many of the men as you can?"

"This is important?"

Jack glanced over his shoulder at the señora who still clung to her dead child.

"I don't want to ever hear a mother crying for her drowned baby again," he said quietly. "If you're going to call a place Esperanza—Hope—it's important for the people who live there to have it."

Jack realized that the people of Esperanza had much to do to make the flooded homes livable again, and so he was surprised two hours later when he followed Mary down below the altar and turned to a crowded sanctuary.

For a moment, all he could see was the grieving señora, barely more than an arm's length away. Hours had passed, and Mary and others had offered repeatedly to prepare her child for burial, and yet the señora sat in the same spot and held fast to the bundled form.

Then Jack scanned the benches and noted the other villagers: the *viejos* with faces like cracked saddle leather, their juniors with features burned dark by the sun, the rebosa-draped women with nursing babies and restless toddlers. Most striking, though, were the muchachos and muchachas, the youths of Esperanza who someday soon would take their elders' places—if this village of hope could only live up to its name.

Jack focused on Mary's pleasing profile as she addressed the gathering.

"I have no husband to speak for me. I have no right to speak on my own. I accept it as our way. I tell you only that Roberto is alive because Jesucristo sent Jack Landon to save him. Twice he saved Roberto, and of all the men in Esperanza, Mister Landon was the one to help the señora who sits here. He is an angel of mercy, thanks be to God, and I ask that you hear him."

Lamenting the undeserved praise, Jack faced a sanctuary full of people whose blank stares told him they were willing to listen.

"I'm tired of seeing people drown." Jack's voice played against the far wall. "What happened last night wasn't the first time here. It won't be the last. There'll be heavy rain again in the watershed. Maybe not for a month, or a year, or ten years, but it's going to happen. The arroyo will get out of banks. More people will drown—some of you, even, or your children. People are going to drown and mothers will keep on crying unless something's done about it."

Mary must have presumed what Jack was about to say, for she touched his arm and nodded for him to turn away with her. When he did so, she leaned close.

"Esperanza is their *patria chica*," she whispered. "You cannot ask them to leave the little fatherland where their grandfathers are buried."

The brush of the señorita's hair against Jack's cheek was not unpleasant. Under other circumstances, he could have wished for the moment to linger, but he quickly faced the crowd again to clear up any misconceptions.

"She reminded me that this is your home," he said. "But you can make it better—safer. I don't know anything about adobe, but I'm sure there's brickmakers among you. You've built walls, good strong walls. You've dug irrigation ditches on the river and used the lay of the land to your advantage, knowing that water always seeks lower ground."

Pausing to formulate his next words, Jack noticed that the blank features in the crowd had given way to squinted eyes and pursed lips. He had their attention.

"Why not build a levee along the arroyo?" he pressed. "An adobe embankment to keep it from flooding? Why not run a ditch off the far side of the arroyo, and channel excess runoff down to the floodplain?"

He watched young and old alike straighten in their seats. Several men looked at one another. A few women whispered among themselves.

Jack had made his point, and the dramatist in him knew better than to belabor the moment. Checking at his shoulder, he found Mary's eyes—dark and intelligent eyes, stunning in their appeal, that seemed like windows into the soul of someone whom his troubled search for purpose would never let him know better.

With almost crushing regret, Jack turned and made his way out the mission doors.

He intended to go through the courtyard arch and never stop until Esperanza and its vexing reminders were as far behind him as the editor and father and girl who would have imprisoned him in a meaningless existence. But something he had seen in Mary's eyes wouldn't let him pass through the graveyard without hesitating. He stood watching a dust devil dance across the graves and shake the leaning crosses, and then he lifted his gaze beyond the crumbling courtyard wall. Hidden in the distance was Mary's home, a place where she and her brother had come so close to drowning, a place where the threat of drowning would always hang over them if the villagers didn't heed Jack's warning.

He went on to the arch, only to stop beneath it with a hand to the curving stonework and look back at the mission. Could he go away without ever knowing to what fate he was leaving her?

Jack lost track of the minutes as he lingered at the spot and waged war with himself. Twice he started away, only to be held in check by something inside him that he couldn't understand. On his third try, he passed through the arch and knew that he had put the mission behind him forever.

But that was before he heard two words carried on the currents.

"Mister Landon?"

The part of him that had lost the inner battle welcomed the voice, and he stopped and turned. Mary was framed by the mission doors behind her, and there was something buoyant in her steps as she approached.

"They have listened," she added, flicking her windblown hair from her cheek. "The *viejos* remember the last flood, and how they had planned to do as you suggest. They remember, too, the days becoming weeks, and the weeks months, and the months years, until they told themselves another flood would never come. Now, because of you, they are determined to make Esperanza a place of hope."

Jack advanced until they stood face-to-face inside the courtyard.

"That's good to hear," he said. "I won't be around to see it, but I hope they follow through this time."

"You are leaving?" There was disappointment in Mary's face.

"I . . ." He glanced over his shoulder and found the world through the arch as empty as ever. "I don't know. I guess."

"It is important you stay, so they will see you every day and not forget their promise."

Still, he hesitated.

"Roberto is not able," Mary added. "I will have to remake my home alone."

She could have said *our* home, thereby including her brother. But she hadn't, and there was something about her choice of the word *my* that made it a personal appeal.

"If there's structural damage, I wouldn't know a thing about it," said Jack.

She merely looked at him with those captivating eyes, and it was easy to choose between service on her behalf and the aimless way through the arch.

"May God bless you for helping."

At Mary's voice, Jack looked up, resting on the upright handle of his rusted shovel in the room where the flood had trapped them. The morning sunlight bursting through the window bathed her face and red headscarf as she leaned over a hoe in the inner doorway. For an hour, as Roberto had rested at the mission, the two of them had bent over their respective implements, piling and then shoveling flood silt out the very window by which they had escaped.

"May God bless you for many things, Mister Landon," she added.

Mister Landon. It was the manner in which the Mexican hands on the ranch had addressed his father, and hearing Mary use it repeatedly was too much a reminder of things better forgotten.

"Name's Jack. With what we went through, we ought to be on a first-name basis."

Mary gave a relaxed smile. "You are from a different place, and your customs are different."

"*Life* was different where I'm from. The things I know about are different."

"I hear your words in two languages and can tell you are educated."

Jack readjusted his grip on the shovel. Shortly after high school, he had hired on at the *Daily Standard* rather than matriculate at a college.

"Higher academics never was of much interest to me," he said. "What I know's more a by-product of the job I was in."

"Oh?"

"Sort of a continual learning experience, I guess. You can't write about something if you don't do the homework to understand it."

As soon as he said the words, Jack wished he hadn't broached the profession he had fled.

Her eyebrows rose. "You are a writer, Jack Landon?"

He would have deflected the question, but his name on her voice pried open a part of him that he would have kept closed.

"I was with a newspaper."

She placed a finger under her lip in apparent reflection before her face took on more energy. She leaned the hoe against the doorjamb and spoke as she came nearer.

"When the older students still came to school, their teacher would tell them they must learn to read and write English."

Just a few days ago, Jack would have agreed, but now he wasn't so sure. In a world so futile, maybe he was no better off with all his skills than a peon farmer in this jumping-off place to nowhere.

But he wasn't going to say it out loud. Instead, he followed up by asking, "So your brother's not in school?"

"There is no one to teach him. Their teacher took his family away after the raid at Glenn Springs."

"That was over a year ago. I saw the dispatches out of El Paso."

"He was afraid for his wife and children. I am afraid too that the revolution will cross over into Esperanza. I worry about our children. I worry about Roberto. He has changed since our father died. I am afraid Villistas or Carrancistas or bandits will try to get him to ride with them. When he was in school, I did not worry."

Pausing, Mary looked expectantly at Jack.

"I have prayed to Our Lady," she said, "for someone to teach the older students."

Jack understood what she proposed, and even as the two of them fell silent and returned to their tasks, her words stayed with him. With every shovelful of silt that he dumped through the window, he pondered this excuse to stay around indefinitely. Again and again, he sneaked glances at Mary as the hoe grated across deposits of sand and gravel. He was more charmed than ever by her rare features, even with streaks of dirt across her cheeks, and he admired the swell of her cotton blouse and the grace with which she carried herself.

"I'm not a teacher," he said abruptly.

She turned and they looked at one another.

"I wouldn't know where to start," Jack added.

Still, she looked him.

"Lesson plans and things like that—I'd be lost," he continued.

Once more, Mary came nearer. "I could help you prepare. The school has books, and the things you know would add to them."

Jack glanced down at his filthy summer suit and the mud-caked boots that had been a snappy two-tone. "All I've got's the clothes on my back."

"The women can make you clothes."

"I don't have a place to stay."

"The school has rooms in back."

"Where the teacher lived?"

"A place for animals too." And then Mary added, as if it would seal the deal, "The people would bring you chickens."

"Chickens?"

Jack repeated it with a chuckle that surprised him. He hadn't thought he would ever find a reason to laugh again.

"And dollars from the county when they do not forget us," she said.

Money meant nothing to Jack anymore, or chickens either, but the one thing that did seem important now was something Mary hadn't mentioned. He studied the beguiling eyes, and

when she responded with a smile, he no longer had a decision
to make.

CHAPTER 8

"I have good news, Roberto."

Several days had passed since the flood, and although the muchacho rested supine on the sanctuary bench, he was alert and his cough had subsided. In prayer for him, Mary had just lighted a votive candle near the altar, and she seemed to feel the flame's healing warmth as she eased down beside him and stroked his hair.

"We can go back," she continued in English. "Jack Landon, the man that pulled you from the river, helped prepare our home."

Roberto twisted around to see her. "The gringo?" he responded in Spanish.

There was resentment in his voice, and Mary could see it in the furrows between his eyebrows.

"He is a good man, my brother."

The muchacho's nostrils flared. "No gringo is good."

"Speak English, Roberto. Speak English."

"It's the gringo language. I'm Mexicano."

Mary realized that it might be fruitless to persist in a debate now four months old.

"Without Jack Landon, you would have drowned," she said. "Two times you would have drowned."

Roberto's anger rose, his jaw tightening. "I didn't want the gringo's help. I'm Mexicano."

Mary could smell the hot wax as the votive candle burned; in

63

lighting it, her prayer had been for Roberto to find peace as well as health.

"I would have died too trying to save you," she said. "The padre would now be praying both of our souls out of purgatory if not for Jack Landon."

"To hell with the gringo. Let him burn in *infierno* with the gringo that killed our papá."

The boy turned away, but not before Mary could see his eyes glisten and reflect the glow of the candle. Her own eyes began to sting, for the pain of loss was still strong.

"Not every white man is bad, Roberto. Did the padre not talk to you? There are good whites and bad whites, just like there are good Mexicans and bad Mexicans."

Still, Roberto wouldn't face her. "So why didn't the good whites punish the one that killed Papa? They're all bad!"

Mary didn't want to upset Roberto while he was fragile, so she said nothing. Besides, how could she explain what she couldn't understand herself? Day after day, she had visited their father's grave just outside the mission doors, and still she had no answers.

"Think what Papa would have wanted for you," she finally said. "He was proud that I learned English so well from the other padre when I was young. Papa knew we cannot stay in the little fatherland forever."

Roberto turned and raised himself to his elbows. "So he took his burro loads of candelilla somewhere else, and the gringo buyer killed him! I won't ever leave the *patria chica*—except to kill gringos!"

"Do not say that, Roberto," She motioned to the crucifix beyond the altar. "Look, Jesucristo looks down on you. Please, do not say that!"

"He let Papa die. Maybe Jesucristo only watches over gringos."

"No, Roberto, no. He has thoughts of peace for you, and not evil."

For a long while, the two of them sat in silence as the votive candle burned with a soft crackle. There was something else Mary wanted to discuss, but she didn't know if this was the time.

"You are going back to school," she heard herself say.

Once more, the muchacho looked at her. "There's nothing you can teach me."

"There is a new teacher. The elders and padre are in favor. Now the boys your age will learn again."

"I have a man's things to do."

"A man should know English. He should speak it and write it if he is to be everything he can be."

It was the same tack that Mary had tried with her brother for months, and his response was no different than before.

"*Español* was good enough for Papa. It's good enough for me."

"No, no, no, Roberto. English is what sets us apart as Americans. The Rangers and Army look at Esperanza and wonder if we are for the Carrancistas or Villistas. They wonder if maybe the bandits that attack the ranches are from Esperanza. English will set us apart from the revolutionaries and keep us from being suspected. We should all speak English like the whites so we will have their trust."

"I don't want their trust!" cried the boy. "I want them to die!"

Mary's heart bled for Roberto, and she tried to comfort him by stroking his hair again. But the youth recoiled from her touch.

"How can you want to be in the gringo world?" he demanded.

"There is not a world for whites and another one for Mexicans, my brother. We are all together."

"Tell that to the gringos. They'd laugh at you! They use us

and then kill us when they don't need us anymore. For Papa, I'll get back at them!"

"That would only bring shame to our father. He raised us to follow Jesucristo, not the evil one."

For months, Mary had tried to reach a part of Roberto that had seemed to die with their father, and now, as he turned away once more, she worried that she might never be able. But maybe she could still appeal to him as the surrogate mother she had always been.

"You will go back to school to honor Papa," she said in a tone that not only expected compliance, but demanded it. "And your teacher will be Jack Landon."

Mary had never known a flickering kerosene lamp to cast a light so wicked.

It danced like tiny devils in the blue-black steel of the revolver brooding before her on the scarred table. For an hour on this first night home, she had sat staring at the single-action Colt, a dark reminder of all the things that disturbed her about her brother. She could see *Bisley Model 38 W.C.F.* stamped on the four-and-three-quarter-inch barrel, and the pockets of rust in the fluted cylinder. She could see the rearing horse engraved beside the patent date, and a similar representation in the swept-under grip designed for single-hand hold. The hammer had a hollow for a perfect thumb fit, and the trigger was wide and curved to facilitate careful control.

Mary saw all of these things, but the detail that burned strongest in the lamplight were the two letters carved in the butt.

RC.

Roberto's initials.

Alongside the six-shooter was the crumpled chamois pouch with its drawstring loose, and the devil lights also skulked inside among the jumbled cartridges. The brass shell casings were tarnished above the rims, but Mary knew that the bottlenecked slugs at the muzzle ends could discolor in a way that would leave someone dead.

She prayed to Jesucristo that it wouldn't be Roberto.

"That's mine!"

To the exclamation in Spanish, a hand darted out from behind and dragged the revolver away from the lamp. Almost as quickly, Mary pinned the hand and weapon against the table.

"What is *this*, Roberto?" she demanded, finding him at her shoulder.

"It's mine, I said!" The boy wouldn't make eye contact.

"Where did you get it? Why do you have it?"

"That's *my* business, Marita. *My* business."

"You live under the roof of our father and his father. They worked hard and were honest and respectful. Just because they are gone does not mean you can dishonor them."

Roberto wriggled his hand free of Mary's, but the revolver still lay on the table when he withdrew his arm.

"Where have you kept it?" the youth pressed. "You had no right to go through my things!"

"You thought the flood took it. I wish the water *had* carried it away."

Roberto didn't respond, but sinister shadows seemed to play in his face.

"While you slept," Mary continued, "I have pleaded with Our Lady for you. Has the evil one led you into trouble? What use do you have for this revolver?"

"I want it back!"

"Answer my questions, Roberto. Tell me also why you were across the river when the water was high."

"Let me have my *pistola*, or I'll find it when you're asleep."

Mary tightened her hand on the weapon that still rested on

the table. "You almost drowned in the river. What business did you have in Mexico?"

Roberto only stood there, his ears flushing as he firmed up his jaw.

"You know what the people of Esperanza say," continued Mary. "They say the Carrancistas or Villistas or bandits try to get the boys on the river to join them. The *capitáns* want them to ride against the white Americans on the ranches and settlements. They burn their homes and steal payrolls from the mines. They kill innocent people."

"No gringo is innocent!"

Mary shuddered. "Tell me you would not do such a thing. You are American, just like the white Americans they rob and kill."

"I'm Mexicano! I'll always be Mexicano because of what the gringos did to Papa!"

The boy stormed away, leaving Mary to stare again at the ungoldly lights dancing in the revolver's cold steel. He had neither confirmed nor denied her fears, but she knew that if ever there was a youth open to the deviltry of border rogues, he would be someone like Roberto.

And there wasn't a thing she could do about it, except ask Our Lady to intercede on her brother's behalf.

CHAPTER 9

"Here, chick, chick, chick."

With a lilting call into the morning sun and a handful of shelled corn from a burlap bag, Jack drew the attention of the roaming chickens. As he broadcast the corn across bare ground outside a ramshackle coop under the yucca hill and summit cross, the hens clucked and ran to him. Prancing about, they nodded and pecked, finding kernel after kernel as their white feathers ruffled and the red wattles shook under their beaks. As the ground turned bare again, they looked at him curiously, begging for more, and he obliged with another handful of kernels.

Jack was fascinated, watching the chickens as he never had back on the ranch. Indeed, here on Esperanza's northeast edge, a hundred yards along the base of the hill from the mission, life seemed fresher in every way today, and he was strangely content as he stood with his back to the mud-brick walls of the uncultured school addition that was now his home. He had spent his first night in it, and he had slept the best he had in a long time.

True to Mary's prediction, townspeople had brought chickens. But Jack hadn't been prepared for the reins of a dapple gray horse that her elderly friend, Longino Castaneda, had delivered to his door. Jack had politely refused, but the *viejo* had promised that the horse would be available whenever Jack needed it.

Other townspeople had brought loose-fitting, white cotton garments and leather sandals, and Jack dressed very much the part of a villager as he waded through the hens to the small coop yard. Framed by cured ocotillo stalks, the mesh-wire fencing was essential to protect against night-prowling varmints while the poultry roosted.

Avoiding the fresh excrement, he entered through the open gate and found the shallow water basin polluted with down. He would need to refill it before the sun rose much higher.

Inside the hen house, which was also gated, the angling roost ladder was askew, and Jack was about to straighten it when he heard footsteps behind him. Turning, he checked through the chicken wire and saw Mary approaching with a couple of items wrapped in white cloth.

"Buenos días," said Jack, starting toward her.

"I pray the angels brought you rest, Jack Landon."

As the two of them met outside where the chickens fed, Mary extended one of her burdens. "I prepared tortillas for you."

Half the village must have cooked tortillas, thought Jack, for he had awakened to the universal sound of villagers slapping dough into thin cakes. But he didn't complain as he accepted a warm, covered dish that exuded so pleasant an aroma that his stomach growled.

"Gracias, Señorita Mary. I can't think of a better breakfast." He looked down and tugged on his peon garments. "I guess I'm assimilating in lots of ways. 'When a man doth to Rome come, he must do as there is done.' "

Clearly puzzled, Mary turned her head sideways.

"Lo siento," apologized Jack before continuing in Spanish. "It's from a sixteenth-century play by Henry Porter. It means to accommodate yourself to local customs when you're new to a place."

"I am glad you are here, Jack Landon," she said, choosing

70

not to respond in Spanish. "If you come to my house in afternoon, I will help you with lesson plans. But if I do not offend you, I wish you to speak only English."

He obliged. "I guess if I'm to teach its finer points, I need to do that, all right."

"It is more than about what you teach. Esperanza is in a dangerous place. We are caught between the Carrancistas, Villistas, and bandits on one side, and the white ranchers, rangers, and soldiers who do not know if they can trust us. I wish everyone in Esperanza would speak English."

Jack nodded. "A good way to show your loyalties. It's human nature to trust somebody better if they talk like you instead of the riffraff."

"The elderly people in Esperanza speak only Spanish. They are too old to be a threat. But I worry about the strong young men, and the boys who will be men. People say that the armies across the river try to get them to ride against American mines and ranches. The Rangers and Army have reason to suspect Esperanza."

"As collaborators," said Jack, the dynamics becoming clear. "I can see why you'd want to hear only English from the men and older boys."

"Yes, boys like my brother."

Mary's features went wry in uncertainty, and she unwrapped the second item to reveal a bulky chamois pouch. Loosening the drawstring, she withdrew a revolver and let it rest in her palms, the blue-black steel stark against the draping white cloth. The sunlight winked in its fluted cylinder and four-and-three-quarter-inch barrel, and there was something unsettling in the way Mary eyed the weapon before she looked up.

"It is Roberto's." Her voice trembled. "He will not say where it got it. He will not say why he was across the river when you saved him from drowning."

Jack understood her concern. "High as the water was, he had to feel pretty strong about something to cross it like he did."

Mary's eyes began to glisten. "Our father is dead, months ago now. It changed Roberto."

Even at twenty-five, Jack was still trying to cope with the loss of a parent. "It takes a long time to work through grief."

"It is more than grief. It is bitterness against gringos—even you, Jack Landon."

Waiting, Jack remembered Roberto's odd behavior toward him from the moment he had revived the muchacho beside the river.

"Our father hauled candelilla wax on his burros," the señorita continued. "From the time he was young he did this. He liked everyone, and everyone liked him. In the spring he and Roberto took his wax to a new buyer, a white man. When the man would not pay a fair price, our father started away and the buyer shot him. The white man took the wax and our father died in Roberto's arms."

"Good God."

Suddenly Jack could see nothing but a boy's white cotton weave soaking up his father's blood.

"What did the law do?" he asked.

Mary began to blink a lot and she hung her head. It was the kind of picture Jack had always filed away to use later in conveying emotion to the reader, but this time he thought only of offering an embrace. He might have done so, but she seemed to find new strength and straightened.

"Do you know what many white people call us, Jack Landon?"

Jack knew a couple of the pejoratives: pepper bellies and greasers. His father had casually tossed the terms around when discussing his Mexican ranch hands.

"People can come up with all kinds of names for somebody different from them," he said. "I guess it's always been that way—class divisions based on things some people think are important."

"I tell Roberto we are all Americans, but he is right. In a white man's court, all that is important is who is white and who is Mexican."

"Is that what happened? They let the buyer get away with it?"

"My brother told the truth. The buyer told lies. The buyer said our father struck him and tried to take his gun. Who were they to believe, a white man, or boy they would call a greaser?"

Jack began to tremble, a surprising rage rising up from inside.

"So the son of a—" He shook his head, not wanting to swear around her. "So the devil walked away scot-free?"

"Ten minutes the jury spent behind the door."

Jack found his fists tightening. "That's not right. It's just not right. They should have hung him."

But he understood why that couldn't have happened. At the *Daily Standard,* he had covered four murder trials, and there had been a conviction in each. Three of the defendants, all of them white, had received sentences of five to twenty years, while the fourth man, a Mexican, had been sent to the gallows for what might have been self-defense.

It was just a part of the unfairness of life, but that didn't make it any easier for Jack to look into Mary's troubled features.

"Will you take this for me, Jack Landon?" She extended the revolver, and Jack accepted, pouch, cartridges, and all.

"So your brother won't have access to it?"

"I am afraid. There are bad men across the river. They raid the American ranches. They steal from the mines. They kill people who have done them no harm. I have prayed to Our Lady that Roberto does not become like them. He has already chosen friends I do not trust, the brothers Román and Natividad."

As Jack studied the Bisley Model, a blemish down behind the

hammer caught his eye. He twisted the revolver in the sunlight, inspecting as the weapon gleamed. There were actually two flaws side by side—shallow marks crudely filed into the steel frame of the grip. From all appearances, they had been freshly made with a hacksaw blade.

Notches.

Jack looked up at Mary. He wondered if his face had paled, because he could feel himself shudder.

"What is wrong?" she asked.

The six-shooter felt unusually heavy. Jack checked the gun again, wondering how carefully she had examined it and whether she would have recognized the significance of the notches. He had once interviewed a retired cattle inspector who had been attached to Company D of the Texas Rangers' Frontier Battalion. The old man had proudly displayed a pearl-handled .41 Colt six-shooter with three notches—one for every man he had killed with it. Jack had felt uncomfortably nervous holding the weapon, and he felt even more so now as he supported Roberto's Bisley and focused on the muzzle.

"Something troubles you?" she asked again.

Jack stuffed the revolver back inside the pouch and tightened the drawstring. She was clearly unaware, and there was no need to make her worry worse.

"I'll keep it for you, Señorita Mary," he said with a forced smile. "I used to shoot rattlers with a .45 growing up on the ranch."

"You have a ranch?"

"My family does. Well, just my father now, since my mother died. I guess I've let loose of the place for good."

"You are strange, Jack Landon."

"Strange?"

"Different. You are educated. You are a writer. Your family has land. And here you are in the clothes of a peon, feeding chickens

74

outside your adobe in Esperanza."

Jack shrugged. "I guess you can have everything and nothing at the same time."

Mary turned for a moment and swept her arm across the panorama of squalid adobe walls hidden away in the Chihuahuan Desert.

"You have come to a place where we have nothing. With your teaching, thanks be to God, maybe our young people can find something someday."

With a parting word, she left, and Jack started for his new home only to hesitate and to dwell on what had just happened. Of all the people in Esperanza, he had been the one who Mary had entrusted with the revolver, and he looked back, watching the feminine swing of her hips.

CHAPTER 10

The striking folds between the knotted eyebrows told Jack everything he needed to know about Mary's brother from across the empty benches of the schoolroom.

Roberto was angry, very angry, and the boy stubbornly paused against the doorway's bright backdrop of morning sunlight and glared at Jack. Then his sister appeared over Roberto's shoulder and ushered him inside, and his ire grew worse. From the front of the room, Jack could hear the boy complain under his breath, but in moments brother and sister were approaching.

"Roberto is ready to learn," said Mary as they stopped before him.

Considering the boy's taut lips and the hard lines that dropped at the corners, Jack hoped never to see Roberto on a day when he *wasn't* ready.

"So what is it you like studying best, Roberto?" Jack asked.

The muchacho only grunted.

"Answer him," prodded Mary.

"If you'll let me know," said Jack, "I'll try to give it special attention."

Still, there was only an uncomfortable silence, until it gave way to Mary's firm, expectant voice.

"Roberto? You must have the respect to—"

"Riding and shooting," interrupted the boy in Spanish with a spiteful glance at his sister. "My caballo is outside."

Jack glanced at Mary, and she glanced at him, and the tension rose between the three of them.

"Well, we won't be doing any of that here," said Jack, not knowing what else to say. "But there's a lot of other things we'll learn. First, though, you'll need to speak English. It's 'horse,' not 'caballo.' Of course, you can keep riding him to school."

Roberto grunted his displeasure and threw out his chest. "School is for children," he said, continuing to speak Spanish. "I'm a man."

"And you think," said Jack, "a man's all about riding and shooting, instead of reading and writing."

Roberto only turned away.

"I want to show you something." Jack held out his hand palm-down, but he couldn't regain the boy's attention. "This scar across my knuckles . . . I was twelve years old and on a cattle drive to the Panhandle with my father. Two weeks out, a bad storm came up at night and the herd stampeded. We all jumped on our horses and took off after them in the dark. You've never heard thunder like the roar of eight hundred steers when they go to running.

"I was riding blind. I couldn't even see my horse's ears. First thing I knew, my horse stumbled and I went down, so close to all those cattle that I could feel the wind coming off their hoofs. One of them stepped on me and scarred this hand. I never even got close to the leaders, much less turned them so they'd start milling. But for a couple of years, I'd look at this scar and think, *Well, I'm a man now.* But I wasn't. I was just a boy with a scarred hand who hadn't gotten the job done."

When Roberto stayed quiet and kept his back to Jack, Mary spoke up.

"Do you hear, my brother? There is a time to be a boy. It is meant to be that way so you can grow in wisdom and in God's favor."

For all of the muchacho's response, she might as well have been talking to the wind.

"One more thing, Roberto," said Jack, despite the boy's refusal to face him. "What seems important to you now might not be important later on. During that cattle drive, all I could think about was being a hand on the ranch. By the time I was fourteen, I didn't have the least interest in it anymore. Like your sister said, I'd grown in wisdom. You need to give yourself time to do the same."

Wisdom.

Where had it been the last few weeks, when Jack could have used it in this lost man's journey of his?

Roberto took a seat, and as more students filed in, Mary drew Jack off to the left, where frayed schoolbooks stood stacked haphazardly against the wall.

"You surprise my brother," she said quietly. "You surprise me, Jack Landon."

"How so?"

"You could not see his face when you were telling the story. *Could feel the wind coming off their hoofs*—is that not how you said it? I had not seen his eyes light up so since our father died."

"He seemed interested in how I framed things?"

"Until he realized that I looked at him. Then he hid it." She probed for a moment with those enchanting eyes. "You are not like anyone I have known, Jack Landon. You have many secrets, and you tell them little by little, like rain dripping off a house."

Jack unexpectedly found himself smiling. But she gave him reason to smile every time she flicked loose strands of midnight-black hair from her graceful cheek.

"Well, I wasn't exactly keeping my cowboy mishap a secret," he said. "Just hadn't had a reason to tell it."

"Roberto and I are the same. He is surprised that someone

who knows so many things was once a vaquero."

"I'm afraid a real vaquero would take issue with somebody calling me one."

"Still, maybe he will listen to your teaching better, knowing that you have ridden in a stampede and could not even see your horse's ears. I think maybe you have gained respect."

"If I have," Jack said doubtfully, "let's hope I keep it once I start teaching. If you hadn't helped me with lesson plans all these weeks, I wouldn't be trying this."

Mary gave him a long look. "You have my respect too, Jack Landon."

Studying Mary in return, Jack had as many unasked questions for himself as for her.

As Jack began reviewing with his seven students to assess their respective levels, Roberto kept his head down except when Jack addressed him directly. As the day wore on, the boy persisted in showing disinterest until Jack moved past English and mathematics to history. Jack had always lamented the lack of local history in the accepted school curriculum, so he was determined to emphasize the events that impacted his students most.

"Carrancistas. Villistas. Bandits." Jack studied Roberto and the six girls. "The river has all three up and down it. Who can tell me why?"

Roberto looked up, but he and his classmates stayed quiet.

"Mounted Inspectors, the U.S. Army, Texas Rangers," continued Jack. "Why are *they* on the river?"

Again, no one replied, but it was clear that even Roberto was absorbed by Jack's questions.

"Raids and shootings and killings," added Jack. "What's it all about?"

Jack paused, writer-like, letting the drama build. With his students' interest piqued, he presented, as simply as he could, the background in Mexico on which all the conflict was built.

He told them of forty years of Mexican presidents and dictators, of elections and mock elections, of forced exile and assassination, of the 1910 call for revolt and the rise of military resistance against those in power. He told of the rebel leaders Venustiano Carranza and Pancho Villa, and of Villa's bitterness when Carranza declared himself president after the two had driven President Victoriano Huerta out of the country in 1914.

To his students' rapt attention, Jack narrated how Villa's forces, or Villistas, fought back in 1915 against Carranza's Constitutionalist Army, or Carrancistas, only to be repelled into northern Chihuahua, the Mexican state across the Rio Grande from Esperanza. He detailed how President Woodrow Wilson announced U.S. support of Carranza, and how Villa retaliated by killing seventeen Americans and attacking Columbus, New Mexico, in 1916.

With Villistas and Carrancistas keeping the border in flames, explained Jack, the unrest had given rise to bandits such as Los Banderos Colorados—the Red Flaggers—who had allegiance to no one. These three hostile factions—bandidos, Villistas, and Carrancistas—made life perilous along the Rio Grande, but there was also a fourth troubling element. The very forces that protected the American side—U.S. Army troops, Customs Mounted Inspectors, and Texas Rangers—were suspicious that villages like Esperanza might be sympathetic to raiders out of Mexico because of their common heritage.

"It's a real worry to some of us," said Jack, with a glance at Mary across the room.

Mary had paused from teaching her own students to listen to Jack's lecture, and now she came forward, the gravity of the matter evident in her features.

"It is as I have told everyone," she addressed the combined classes. "We must speak English to show that we are Americans and not Mexicans. Those who protect the border will hear us speak as they do, and they will trust us more."

Jack studied Mary as she elaborated, and he found himself comparing her to Annie—young, possessive Annie, clinging to him as the crickets had chirped that last night near San Angelo. Character . . . intelligence . . . maturity . . . a sense of responsibility. They were traits displayed best by only one of them, and Jack's admiration grew by the moment.

"I am afraid for Esperanza," concluded Mary. "I am afraid for many reasons, but most of all, I am afraid that bandits will turn our brothers and sons against the values of Esperanza."

Scanning the classroom, Jack saw a lot of confusion in the young faces, but only Roberto spoke up. *"¿Por qué?"*

"Remember to speak English, Roberto," said Jack. "To answer your question, bandits might be trying to recruit riders from here in the village. *Recruit* is a good word to know—getting somebody to join a group, or a cause. Now, a cause can be a good thing, but these bandits are the kind of people that would use the boys and men of Esperanza for cannon fodder."

"Cannon . . . ?" asked Roberto.

"Cannon fodder, the least important soldiers, the ones put in danger first. That's what happens when these bandits don't have a cause greater than themselves."

The discussion at an end, Jack and Mary moved on to other matters with their respective students. Jack had much to occupy his attention, but every time he looked at Roberto for the rest of the day, something concerning seemed to linger in the boy's face.

It was late afternoon a mile north of Esperanza, and Roberto ducked under a badly sagging door head and entered the roofless ruins of a rock goatherd hut. Prickly pear grew in the scattered debris, and he picked his way across carefully as the unstable footing crunched underfoot.

"So you are going to that gringo's school?" a voice asked him in Spanish.

On the left, an acne-scarred muchacho, fully grown in size if not in years, looked up from where he squatted with a younger muchacho in the shade of a half-collapsed wall.

"*Sí*," said the second muchacho. "I watched him go in."

Sweat trickled down the larger muchacho's face as he drew on a cigarette. "Why you want to let that white man tell you what to do, like he did all of Esperanza? The flood's gone. I'm tired of working on the new *acequia*, the ditch."

Roberto knew the muchachos well. No one in a village of so few families could fail to know everyone well, but the three of them had a special alliance. Pockmarked Román, almost nineteen, was oldest, and he held Roberto's respect as unofficial *capitán* of the three. He was also the cruelest, and Roberto couldn't count the times that Román had demeaned him. Román's brother Natividad, sixteen, was quieter and less of a brute, but he followed his sibling's lead in everything.

"Give me a cigarette," said Roberto.

Román motioned for him to come closer, and as Roberto did, the older muchacho took a deep drag and laid the half-smoked butt across a cut rock at his knee.

"Take it."

With caution, Roberto did so, but just as he brought the cigarette to his lips, Román cuffed him on the ear, bringing caustic laughter from both brothers. Roberto considered the slap childish of someone he so admired; after all, Román had bragged of riding with bandidos in the attack on Boquillas the year before.

"That gringo not teach you anything?" Román asked.

"Just how to talk like a gringo," spoke up Natividad.

"It's my sister's doing," defended Roberto, his ear smarting.

"Marita says I must go to school."

"*Ay,* Marita," said Román. "Why she never talks to me?"

"She doesn't like you. She says you should work more on the *acequia.* She says you're a wild horse that makes all the tame horses wild."

"Working on the ditch is foolish work. You ready for a man's work like Natividad and me?"

"*Sí.* When will we meet across the *río* again?"

"You practiced with the *pistola?*"

Roberto had worried about this moment ever since Mary had denied him the Bisley. In her absence, he had searched their home, and searched again, and had failed to find it.

"I . . ." Roberto's voice was slow to work. "The water carried it away."

Román rose, his jaw tightening. With his thin face and narrowed eyes, he looked hawklike, and Roberto grew afraid even before Román poked him in the chest.

"I spoke up for you," Román said angrily. "I told Chico Cano you were worthy of the notches cut in the *pistola* by a Villista soldier. What will I say to him? You'll make me look bad."

Roberto retreated a step, stumbling a little. "Pigs and goats washed away. Dogs and cows and burros. The flood took everything. Cano will understand."

"For five years Cano has ridden against the gringos. He's raided *ranchos* and killed mounted inspectors. I was with him when he took what he wanted from the store at Boquillas and carried off the storekeeper. Cano will ask you about the *pistola* he gave you. If he doesn't believe you, he'll kill you."

Roberto began to tremble. It was one thing to lie to Román, but the prospect of doing so to a man like Chico Cano was terrifying.

"What are muchachos like us to Cano?" Roberto asked.

"Chico Cano has no muchachos," said Román. "He has men."

"Men like me and my brother," said Natividad.

But Roberto probed Román more. "Cano's a big *capitán*. What good are we to him?"

"What do you mean?"

"*Sabe* cannon fodder? Will we be the first ones Cano puts in danger to keep the others safe?"

"Cano uses us the way he needs to. Who told you that?"

Roberto hesitated, reluctant to credit a white man in front of his peers.

"Fod . . . How you say? Fodder?" asked Natividad.

"Is that *Inglés,* English?" pressed Román. "That gringo teacher tell you this?"

Roberto didn't want to admit it, so he said nothing.

"You scared, Roberto?" asked Natividad. "Maybe you don't want to cross the *río* no more?"

Roberto thought of his father and found new resolve. "I'll go. Tell me when, and I'll go."

"Saturday," said Román.

"How is it you always know?" asked Roberto.

"An hombre leaves a note in the cottonwood split by lightning."

"The one on the *río*?"

"I spend my free time checking for orders to ride against gringos, while you go to school to a gringo who can't even ride."

"He's not like the other gringo teacher," said Roberto. "Señor Landon was a vaquero when he was twelve, and he rode in a cattle stampede."

"Who told you that?" asked Natividad. "The gringo himself?"

"He was on a drive to some place called the Panhandle."

Román breathed sharply. "You're the gringo's fool. Have you seen him ride? He tells you this to get your respect. Don't you know gringos are liars?"

Roberto turned away, struck by what Román had said. As he remembered and relived, the truth of the muchacho's allegation dawned on Roberto. Whether in a schoolroom or a court of law, gringos were liars, all right, if not murderers.

Roberto faced the muchachos again. "Gringos took Papa's blood. When I ride with Chico Cano, I'll take theirs in return."

CHAPTER 11

Outside the mission courtyard, the coins glinted in the late evening sun of autumn as they dropped with successive clinks into the Texas Ranger's cradled hands.

Standing between a big bay horse and the stone archway, the scruffy ranger accepted the money from the wizened old padre, whose wrinkled face showed concern as he counted out the silver dollars one by one. Looking on from their horses were two other men, equally unkempt in sweat-stained hats and duck trousers, but likewise wearing *cinco peso* badges that identified them as rangers. On horseback in the courtyard was another ranger, similarly distinguished even at a distance by a Colt revolver at his waist and by a bandoleer shining with cartridges across his dusty woolen shirt.

With school over for the day, Jack had started for the arroyo to check the flood control project, but he got no farther than the scene involving the padre, who not only shepherded the mission, but the interests of the village as well. Now, to the barking of dogs suspicious of the strangers, he was delivering into the hands of the ranger silver dollar after silver dollar.

"Padre Diego, *que estas haciendo*?" Jack asked as he approached. "What are you doing?"

The nearby rangers looked at Jack and then turned away dismissively. Clearly, Jack's clothing and fluent Spanish rendered him a peon in their eyes.

"Padre," he asked again, "everything all right?"

This time Father Diego responded with a glance, but when the standing ranger snorted "More," the priest dug into his flowing vestments and brought out another fistful of dollars.

Jack, undaunted by the two riders who suddenly stared down on him, went closer to the transaction and finally drew the undivided attention of both parties.

"What's this about?" pressed Jack, persisting in Spanish. "Why are you giving them money, Padre?"

"It . . ." Father Diego glanced at the man whose cupped hands were poised for more dollars. "It is for Esperanza."

"How so? These men are Texas Rangers."

"*Sí.* They protect us."

Jack studied the ranger—the tight mouth and flaring nostrils and vertical furrows between the eyebrows. He noted also the odd way the man held his head cocked, as if he had a perpetual crick in his neck. As Jack took in these details, the ranger gave him a long look in return. It was a judgmental look, one that said *I'm better than you,* but it was also a hostile look that said *Get the hell out of my face.*

Jack turned from the ranger to Father Diego and back to the ranger, but addressed only the priest.

"They're not making you pay to be protected, are they? That's not what these men are doing, is it?"

The ranger glared at Jack before speaking in English to the two riders alongside. "Get this greaser away from me."

But before the men could react, Jack confronted all three rangers—also in English.

"This *greaser,*" he said sharply, "wants the names of every one of you. Your company and commanding officer too."

The scruffy ranger's jaw dropped as his head jerked back, but he registered no less surprise than the mounted men.

"Who the hell are you?" one of them asked.

"I was a staff writer for the *San Angelo Daily Standard.* If you're trying to extort money from these people to do what the state's already paying you for, I'll have a report on the adjutant general's desk by the end of the week. I'll file the story with the Associated Press, and the governor won't have any choice but to investigate. Now give me your names."

"Ain't telling you nothing," said the scruffy ranger, turning toward his horse.

"The *money*," Jack said in reminder.

The ranger eyed him, and for a moment the two of them stared at one another. In Jack's job, he had challenged his share of individuals and sometimes had met resistance, but never had he seen a glare so intense. As a reporter, Jack had always held his ground out of pride and ego, but this was the first time he had ever done so out of concern for others. Maybe it wasn't wise, crossing armed men who clearly had been conditioned to do as they pleased, but Jack believed the threat of a pen from someone white placed him in the greater position of power.

The ranger threw the silver dollars down in the dust.

"The hell with you," he said, seizing the bay's mane and digging his boot in the stirrup. Once seated, he turned to the courtyard. "Riggs! We're going!"

With a reporter's eye, Jack committed to memory the features of the other two horsemen before the three rode away. One had buckteeth, discolored by tobacco, and a crooked nose that looked as if it hadn't been set properly after a break. The other rider, beetle-browed and thick-necked, was a heavyset man who must have tested his Appaloosa's endurance.

Jack would not soon forget them—and he had no doubt that he had similarly burned a place in their memories.

To the beat of a dozen hoofs, the scruffy ranger looked back over his shoulder. "Riggs!" he called again.

This time, Jack looked past the padre's stooped form to the courtyard, where the rawboned ranger named Riggs and his chestnut horse loomed over the windswept graves and slanting crosses. As the man glanced toward his receding allies, tobacco juice dripped from his tangled red whiskers. Then the chestnut shifted position, and just inside the inverted *V* of the horse's neck and head, Jack saw what he hadn't been able to before: the Señora Ramos kneeling in prayer over a small mound of dirt.

Riggs looked down at her again, and even as Jack passed under the gateway arch, he could hear the ranger proposition her in Spanish mixed with equally vulgar English.

For a moment, Jack relived the aftermath of the flood. He was back in the mission again, watching a distraught figure cling to a dead baby. And as angry as Jack had been about the extortion attempt, it was nothing compared to what he felt now.

"Could you show her some respect?" he asked sharply as he approached. "She's in mourning."

Indeed, from the black rebosa draped over her head to her glistening cheeks and quaking lips, Señora Ramos was the very picture of despondence.

"I got just the thing to take her mind off of it," Riggs said gruffly. "Ain't that right, señora?"

Jack circled around the horse's nose and the newly fashioned cross and came up at the woman's shoulder.

"Señora," Jack said quietly, "you can come back later."

Turning, she looked up with swollen red eyes.

He stretched out his hand. *"Por favor."*

But she was drawn once again to the mound at her knees. *"Mi niño,"* she whispered.

"I know. Here, I'll help you up."

Still, her hand brooded over the grave, and then she withdrew a silvery pendant from her blouse and hung it by its cord from an arm of the cross. It swung there, shining in the sun, and Jack knew enough about Mexican culture to recognize it as a medal dedicated to Saint Jude, the patron saint of lost causes.

Jack wondered how many more lost causes in Esperanza would end the same way.

Now Señora Ramos accepted his hand and stood, but as they started away, Riggs turned his horse across their path.

"Quit your damned buttin' in," he snapped. "I ain't done with her."

Jack took the woman by the arm and tried to escort her around the horse, but the ranger blocked them as before. Again, Jack and the señora swung wide, only to face eight hundred pounds of muscled animal.

This was about to turn ugly, and Jack knew it. He had learned a lot about human nature as a reporter, and he recognized that this was the kind of man who might not be cowed by the threat of a report or a news story. He looked too damned mean, and his forty-five was too close at hand.

The mission doors were behind them now, thirty yards away, and Jack bent close to Señora Ramos.

"Get inside and bolt the doors," he whispered. "*Vaya con prisa.* Quick."

The moment she started for the mission, Riggs's face turned dark. "Get back over here." he ordered. "No whore's runnin' off from *me* that away."

He squeezed his horse with his thighs to give chase, but Jack seized the animal by the cheek of the bridle.

"What the hell!" exclaimed Riggs.

Jack held fast as the chestnut tossed its head. "Just leave her alone," he said quietly, hoping a calm demeanor would defuse the situation.

"Let loose!"

Jack checked over his shoulder and gauged the retreating señora's position. Just a few more seconds and she would reach the rock approach outside the mission doors.

But suddenly there was an ominous *click-click,* and Jack spun back to stare into the muzzle of the ranger's cocked .45.

"Only thing worse than a pepper belly's a Meskin lover," said Riggs.

Jack had faced plenty of tense moments as a reporter, but this was the first time he had been a twitch of a finger from taking a bullet. Even now, he didn't think Riggs would shoot, but that didn't mean that Jack hadn't placed himself in legal jeopardy. He fully expected the ranger to take him into custody on a trumped-up charge, and in an area where prejudice was so powerful, could there be any more justice in a matter involving the señora than in the murder of Mary's father?

Jack released the bridle. "All right, he's loose."

Riggs lowered his revolver and gigged the horse for the mission. Taking a direct course in callous disrespect for the dead, he let the chestnut bowl over three crosses and trample the graves in his haste to overtake the señora. Nevertheless, she was safely inside by the time he pulled rein at the closed doors. From the saddle, the ranger leaned over to swing them wide, as if determined to ride inside, and even at a distance, Jack could hear the profanity spew when the doors wouldn't give.

Riggs still had the .45 in his hand, and he beat on the heavy wood with the butt and yelled for the woman to come out. Between the shouting and the swearing and the strike of shifting hoofs on rock, it was a scene that would have bordered on blasphemy had Jack believed in that sort of thing.

Confident that the doors would hold, Jack casually started away, defying an instinctive urge to run. Maybe if he showed no expectation of reprisal, the ranger would ignore him when he abandoned his lewd notions. Nevertheless, Jack made it only a few steps past the courtyard arch before the commotion ended and hoofbeats rose up from behind.

Riggs leveled a vicious epithet on him, but Jack didn't break stride until the ranger spoke again.

"I'm talkin' to *you*, Meskin lover."

Turning, Jack watched Riggs duck under the arch and rein up, leaving himself perfectly framed by the vaulted stones. For a moment, the two of them considered one another, and then the ranger spat a stream of tobacco juice that pitted the dust at Jack's feet.

"Cross me again and there'll be hell to pay, you SOB."

Riggs spurred the chestnut and the animal was away, its hoofs churning the loose soil.

All this time, Father Diego had looked on from just outside the courtyard wall, and Jack approached him after a final glance at the rising dust. The old padre seemed more stooped than before, and he had lost color in his face.

"How long's this been going on?" Jack asked.

Father Diego's lips trembled, but he didn't answer.

"The money," said Jack. "How long have they been making you pay?"

"I am afraid," the padre whispered. "I am afraid for Esperanza."

"Those men draw money from the state. They don't have any right to take it from you."

"*Sí*, but Señor Wolfe and the others are bad. They are very bad."

"That the one in charge? Wolfe? They've been threatening you? Is that what they've been doing?"

The old priest turned toward the adjacent plaza and the hidden river, the direction in which the rangers had withdrawn. They had disappeared behind the adobes, but the dust from their horses still plumed up over the thatch roofs.

"They will come back." Father Diego's voice quavered. "*Ay Dios*, Fox, *capitán* of Company B, he will send his eleven *hombres* back, and I must pay them twice as much."

Bending over, he scratched in the dirt and uncovered a silver dollar.

Jack joined him in the search and uncovered a tarnished coin. "You shouldn't pay them a red cent. It's extortion, plain and simple."

"They will punish us. They will burn Esperanza to the ground."

Stunned, Jack stood upright. "They told you that? They actually threatened that kind of thing?"

Father Diego only continued to dig at his feet, a shrunken figure more vulnerable than ever.

It was the first time Jack had ever kneeled before a cross.

Fashioned from sotol stalks, it had adorned the grave of the señora's baby, but now it was down in the dirt, razed by a ranger's profane ride across the courtyard. The leather tie string was loose, and as Jack stood the marker upright, the transverse section tilted and the dangling Saint Jude's medal slipped off. He set about making repairs, first removing the binding and then rewrapping, weaving the strap in and out of the four right angles.

Jack had never read the Gospels, but by osmosis he had gathered that Jesus, known as the Christ, had died by Roman crucifixion. Still, he had never understood the reverence for two lengths of wood joined transversely. Regardless, the structure was clearly important to people like Mary, and for a moment on this troubling search of his for something indefinable, he almost envied her.

With the cross mended, he reached for the Saint Jude's medal in the dirt at his knee, only to see a dainty hand beat him to it. Looking up, he saw Mary kneeling beside him, her dark hair falling gracefully across her cheek.

"I was just thinking about you," he said.

She had still been at school when Jack had left, but he knew that her walk home would have naturally brought her this way.

"What happened, Jack Landon?" She lifted her gaze to the flattened crosses leading to the mission. "There are more."

Jack recounted the events.

"It is as I have said." Mary began to weep. "We are not worthy of their trust or protection. We are only greasers to—what is the word?"

"Exploit," said Jack.

She dabbed at her cheeks. "I did not know the padre had done this. I am sad for him. I am sad for Esperanza." She looked down at the medal in her hand. "And I am sad for Señora Ramos."

Jack considered all that Mary had said as they set the cross in its rightful place at the grave's head. As they worked in close quarters, their arms touched, and the pleasantness of the contact affirmed the growing bond Jack felt with her.

"The idea of appeasement . . ." Jack was strangely eager to confide in her, as if doing so would bring them closer. "Did I do the wrong thing, challenging those rangers?"

"Our people work hard for the money they give to the Church," she said. "It is not right for someone to take it. I am proud that you stood up to them for the padre . . . for Esperanza . . ."

He seemed to read so many things in her eyes as she added five words.

"And for me, Jack Landon."

He wanted to pull her close and wipe away the glistening beads that had squeezed out between her eyelids. He wanted to tell her that everything was all right, that all her tomorrows would be all right. And he wanted to hear her say the same things in return, for inside him was still a hollow, and nothing seemed to fill it.

Mary slipped the Saint Jude's medal over the arm of the cross, and they moved on to the next defiled grave, and then to the one after that. Throughout, it seemed to Jack that the unspoken between them was more powerful than what they actually said. Finally, with the last cross restored, Mary stood in place, as if she was as reluctant to go her separate way as Jack was to see her go.

"I am sad, Jack Landon," she said again.

Maybe it was a hint that she needed his embrace, and maybe it wasn't, but clearly she didn't want to be alone. Regardless, with sunset imminent and the rangers still in the area, there was no way Jack would let her back on the street by herself.

"Let me go inside and get Señora Ramos and we'll walk her home," he said.

They escorted the señora without incident to her adobe, where Jack waited outside as night fell while Mary attended the grieving woman. Her ministrations completed, Mary seemed pleased to have Jack alongside as they continued on for her home, for she stayed so close that their arms sometimes brushed.

When they stopped before her adobe and faced one another, the shadows lay heavy across her features, but that didn't keep Jack from searching the star glow in her eyes. A chorus of crickets rose up from the night, a serenade louder than any since his last moments with Annie on her family's farm. How long ago that seemed now. How far away and how different that life had been. Or maybe it was Jack who had changed—and was still changing, little by little.

Abruptly, he found Mary edging closer.

"I am sad, Jack Landon," she whispered, echoing her earlier words. "But I am also happy."

She gave him a hug that startled him, and sustained it for long seconds before she disappeared into her home.

★ ★ ★ ★ ★

Jack sat and stared into a kerosene lamp at his home and lived again Mary's embrace.

He could feel her head in the hollow of his neck, and her curves warm against his chest. He could smell the freshness of her hair, and took pleasure in the caress of buoyant tresses against his cheek. Under his hands, he could feel the tremble in the back of her shoulders—whether a shiver of fear or excitement, he didn't know, although he experienced a similar sensation.

Indeed, that moment outside Mary's adobe had warranted as much apprehension in Jack as it had elation, for he realized that something was happening between them. Could he risk being imprisoned in as narrow a world as before? A life in which others would dictate just who and what he was to be? How could he chance it, when his search remained unfulfilled?

But that embrace . . .

He couldn't ignore what it had meant to him, and how much he wished it had lingered even longer.

Jack was glad that he had another task to occupy his mind tonight, and he bent over a writing tablet at a table and crafted a letter to the adjutant general in Austin. To the dancing shadow of his pen, he related the incidents outside the mission. He didn't have all of their names, but with a reporter's eye for detail he carefully described the four rangers and related what had been said. A single letter might not have impact, but it would be a powerful record in case the same rangers committed subsequent offenses.

He then crafted a news report with the headline "Who Are the Real Bandits?" and signed it "Border Correspondent." This, he addressed to the *El Paso Morning Times*, which, despite his threat to the ranger, would be more likely to pick up an anonymous letter than would the Associated Press.

Anonymous.

For a writer who had reveled in seeing his name in print, Jack was surprised to realize how much his newfound anonymity meant to him.

His reports finished, all that remained now was to go downriver Saturday and mail the letters at the store in Candelaria. Jack had been told that a mail hack made regular trips from that border outpost, up the rugged Candelaria Rim to the Brite Ranch under Capote Peak, and on to the Southern Pacific Railroad at Marfa.

For the first time, Jack was glad that old Longino Castaneda had insisted on making a dapple gray saddle horse available for his use.

Although Jack was passionate about ending the rangers' misconduct, neither silver dollars nor lewd remarks were on his mind as he stretched out in bed that night. On the contrary, he drifted off to sleep reliving once again the fragrance of buoyant tresses and the warmth of graceful curves.

CHAPTER 12

From the stirrups of the dapple gray along the Candelaria road at sunrise, Jack looked through the black willows and tall cane at the Rio Grande ford and saw a receding horse splash through the far shallows.

There was something familiar about that roan, its wet coat burnished by the rays as it climbed the opposite bank, and about its rider as they disappeared in the paloverde trees. Even viewed from behind and across the golden river, the rider was almost certainly who Jack feared he might be.

Back in August, Jack had fortuitously happened upon him returning from Mexico, and now the muchacho may have reentered that land of revolution and banditry. For a moment, Jack was unsettled by the memory of a worried Mary extending the Bisley Model Colt, freshly notched in two places, which Jack now wore inside his rope belt. Of further concern was the fact that, after the progress he had believed he had made with Roberto on the first day of school, the muchacho had sat sullenly in the weeks that had followed. Clearly, the boy was still emotionally disturbed and open to the wrong influences.

They were reasons enough for Jack to turn his horse away from the road and take the animal through the cane and willows and down into the *río's* gentle ripples. His only reason for bringing the revolver had been to bolster his confidence in light of the Texas Ranger presence in the area; the threat by Riggs was still fresh on his mind. But as Jack bore toward bandit country, he was glad to have the weapon.

When he reached the thick paloverdes on the Mexico bank, he drew rein and parted the needle-leafed branches. In moments he confirmed that it was indeed Roberto who pulled away across the floodplain, the sand powdering up from the roan's hoofs and hanging against a blue-gray backdrop of distant crags. Jack waited until the muchacho dropped out of sight at a wall of brush and then followed.

He tracked Roberto down into badlands that demanded a twisting course through arroyos lined by screwbean and mesquite, over rocky ridges laced with lechuguilla, and past buttes where Spanish daggers stood against the sky. Jack had no intention of riding the boy down and asking where he was headed; the muchacho almost certainly would refuse to tell him. Jack was content to lag out of sight, hoping to learn something clandestinely that would reassure Mary.

But that wasn't Jack's only motivation. He had come to feel empathy for this boy who seemed as lost as he and who likewise struggled for peace.

After holding to the trail for almost an hour, Jack found himself in a gulch with high, steep bluffs. Sandy and serpentine, the drainage deadened the dapple gray's hoofbeats, while simultaneously concealing what lay around every dogleg. Advancing with caution toward a sharp bend to the left, he was about to bare himself to the next straightaway when he heard voices.

Jack pulled rein and froze. There were men ahead, and whoever they were, they were close—too close. He backed his horse a dozen steps and dismounted, careful not to rattle the saddle. A red-berried algerita shrub grew against the left bluff, and he secured the reins to the stem and looked up at the intimidating slope. Void of vegetation, it rose sixty feet and ended at blue sky, and through this wall lay the source of the voices he had heard.

What am I getting myself into?

The question came to Jack as he shed his sombrero and began scrambling up, his fingers clawing at hard-packed earth and his leather sandals slipping. The revolver dug into his pelvis as he wormed his way, fighting for every inch. Eventually he sprawled on the summit, a bulging hogback no wider than his body.

Below, in a hollow where the gulch forked, three Mexican riders surrounded Roberto on his roan. The men were unkempt, with stained sombreros and dark, scraggly whiskers, and even from Jack's high position, he could smell the reek of their sweat. The stocks of carbines showed in their saddle scabbards, while cartridges filled their crisscrossed bandoleers or midriff belts.

Maybe Roberto had intended to rendezvous with bandidos, and maybe he hadn't, but he clearly was being met by threat. Everyone talked over one another, but the word Jack kept hearing was *caballo*—horse—and when one Mexican clutched the roan's bridle and another shoved a revolver in the muchacho's face, the situation grew desperate.

Jack drew the Bisley. These were men who might not stop with taking Roberto's horse; they appeared almost certain to kill him. And yet Jack knew that if he opened fire, the situation would escalate and might cost him his own life.

Mary.

How much she had come to mean to him in so short a time. Could he turn away, knowing the grief she would carry forever?

Bracing his gun arm along the hogback's descending slope, Jack looked down the four-and-three-quarter-inch barrel. With a *click-click*, he thumbed back the hammer and captured the *pistola*-wielding bandit and his bay horse in the wavering sight. Hesitating, he saw the reflection of light in the Bisley's loading gate and felt the concave trigger against his finger. Jack had been a writer, not a soldier, and he knew that this was a situation from which he wouldn't be able to write his way out.

As if someone else controlled his actions, he fired.

The Bisley roared through the hollow, the recoil throwing his arm back. The bandit's bay dropped to its knees and went down, taking the Mexican with it. The other horses went wild in alarm. The report still reverberated as two mounted brigands and Roberto whirled in Jack's direction.

Jack fired again, this time with a shout.

"Roberto! Get out of there!"

A second horse staggered with its Mexican rider. A revolver flashed in the sun and came up from the ground, and so did a carbine from a saddle scabbard.

The muchacho seized control of his roan, and an instant later he had the animal bolting back down the gulch for the bend. Simultaneously, a carbine boomed and dirt exploded beside Jack's elbow. Rolling away with a cry, he lost his balance. Abruptly, he was on his back and sliding down the way he had come, the packed earth taking the hide off his back and hips.

Unable to slow his descent, Jack could only try to avoid a tumble that might disable or kill him. He kept his legs below him and spilled out into the algerita where his horse was secured. Crashing through, he rolled up against the dapple gray's hoofs and frightened the animal. He was afraid the horse would break free, but the shrub held long enough for Jack to gain his feet and untie the reins.

A roan surged by, throwing sand with every muffled hoofbeat. From its saddle, Roberto looked over as Jack swung across his own mount, and then the muchacho was leading him in a desperate flight down the gulch.

They veered left with a dogleg, moments before a carbine cracked from behind. Maybe Jack had put two of the bandits' horses out of commission, but a single armed rider could kill just as surely.

What a story this would make.

Even now, as scared as he was, Jack couldn't shed the mindset of a writer. But when another rifle shot chased him down a straightaway and added to his dread, he realized anew why no reporter had a right to consider someone else's moment in hell as fodder for a worthless award-winner.

Although Roberto's lesser weight gave his roan an advantage, he didn't have the experience of Jack, who had learned to ride under the guidance of men who had cowboyed far and wide. The muchacho did all right where the course was straight, but Jack's superior horsemanship allowed him to navigate bends much more tightly. With every turn, Jack had to hold the dapple gray to avoid a collision, even as his glances back revealed a bandit steadily gaining. Soon, the Mexican would catch them in an open stretch where the carbine would do its job.

Maybe it was time for Jack to draw upon a writer's ability to place himself in a scene that was yet to happen.

In the creative corner of his mind, he experienced two potential moments. One would issue from persisting in flight and waiting for the consequences. The other would proceed from putting into motion daring action. The former was foredoomed, while the latter . . .

Jack could already feel and hear what that second option would bring. He could smell it and taste it, but most vivid were all the things he would see, the little details that together would make up the greater picture.

Just around the next dogleg to the right, Jack converted imagination into reality. Pulling rein so forcefully that the dapple gray almost sat on its haunches, he threw the animal up against the right bank and held it there, the Bisley cocked and ready. The sand rose up bitter and thick, and to the rumble of hoofs navigating the turn, a brute object exploded through it.

Jack fired at nearly point-blank range. To a loud squeal, the dark shape dropped with an upheaval that Jack could feel through the saddle. The thing plowed through the ground, and with it went a smaller figure, ghostly as it flashed through the sandstorm. Jack fired again and turned his horse down the gulch, and in moments the dapple gray was in a gallop as he leaned into the flying mane and asked the animal for everything it had to give.

This was a long, exposed section, and it would have been deadly if the situation hadn't changed. Even so, Jack was still in harm's way when another rifle shot shook the bluffs and a ricochet whizzed past, too close for comfort. Then the dapple gray negotiated a bend to the right and Jack was no longer in the line of fire.

He was almost certain that he had ended the bandits' capacity to pursue on horseback, but he nevertheless kept the dapple gray in a run. Soon he caught up with Roberto, and only after they climbed from the gulch and entered the badlands did they walk their white-lathered horses.

"You rode in cattle stampede, like you say," the boy said in his halting English. "When you a muchacho, you rode same way in cattle stampede."

Roberto showed his surprise for Jack's riding skill by more than words; as they came abreast, his head tilted forward so that he looked up admiringly at Jack from an even lower perspective.

"The experience came in handy, I guess," said Jack as their mounts nodded along. "Never thought I'd be in a firefight."

"You ride like vaquero," the muchacho persisted. *"Madre de Dios."*

But Jack had another matter on his mind. "Roberto, why do you want to get mixed up with men like those?"

"They are horse thieves. I already have caballo." The muchacho patted the roan's neck.

"So you didn't know them? They're not with Los Banderos

Colorados, the Red Flaggers?"

"The Colorados fight for what theirs," replied Roberto. "They don't take hombre's horse."

The muchacho clearly thought more highly of the Colorados than he should have.

"How you know so much about the Colorados?" pressed Jack. "What business do you have being over here?"

But Roberto turned the question back on Jack. "Why you follow me?"

"I didn't start out to. I was headed to Candelaria when I saw you cross the river. It's a good thing I did—those men meant to kill you."

"*Sí.*" The muchacho lowered his gaze, and when he looked up there was acrimony in his words. "You're a gringo. Why you care if they kill me?"

"You're my student and friend. What other reason would I need to watch out for you?"

"You want my sister like she a whore. You want Marita pay you back like a whore."

Jack had just come face to face with bandits set on killing, and yet he was more stunned by what Roberto had said. Involuntarily, he reined up, inducing the muchacho to do the same.

"Roberto, I like your sister. I like her a lot. She's smart and pretty and cares about people. Never for a moment have I thought of her the way you're saying."

"You're a gringo. All gringos want Mexican señoritas for whores."

"Not this one. I admire your sister more than you can imagine. She's got my respect, and so do you."

They rode on, and for a while the only sounds besides hoofs grinding loose rock were the rustle of varied buntings in scrub mesquites and the frenetic, two-note calls of blue quail.

Throughout, Roberto must have pondered Jack's words, for there was surprising eagerness in the muchacho's voice when he spoke again.

"You rode in cattle stampede. Tell again how you felt the wind of their hoofs."

Maybe Jack was making progress with the boy after all.

This time, Jack added all the details he had left out about that night: the big blow and punishing hail, the sonorous thunder and the clash of horns, the beat of his horse's heart against his leg, and the eerie ghost fires on the animal's ears. There had been an engine of destruction at work that night, a dark, twisting rope dropping out of the sky and showing in flashes of wicked lightning. And throughout, young Jack had clung to his mount until a prairie dog hole or jutting rock had felled them both.

After what had happened today, he had escaped a shallow grave twice now—no, three times, for there also had been the flooded arroyo where he had left his mother to die.

Again, they lapsed into silence, and this time it lasted until they left the badlands and entered open desert that stretched toward Rio Grande greenery.

"My sister say you are a good man," said Roberto, abreast on Jack's left.

Convicted by his shortcomings, Jack shrugged as he looked ahead over the dapple gray's ears. "I've got my faults. But that's nice of her to say."

"Marita like you, the way a señorita like a man."

Taken aback, all Jack could do was turn to him.

"She talk about you all the time," Roberto continued.

As much as Jack had longed before for Mary's embrace, he now ached for her arms around him.

"I . . ." Jack searched for the right response. "Going through a flood like we did can make people feel close sometimes."

"She say we would be *muertos*, dead, if you not there. Like me today."

Jack didn't know what to say, but Roberto did.

"Maybe you not same as other gringos. Maybe you care."

Jack studied the muchacho gently rocking against a backdrop of twisted Spanish daggers.

"I'm sorry what happened to your father. I'm sorry the court didn't bring closure for you or your sister. There's a lot of injustice I wish I could do something about."

"You have a *pistola—my pistola*. Give it back and I will do something about it."

Jack glanced at the Bisley and then looked the teenager squarely in the eyes. "Tell me why it's notched, Roberto."

"*¿Qué?*"

"On the frame below the hammer. Two places. I think you know what I'm talking about."

The boy looked away.

"You shoot and kill somebody, Roberto? You riding with the Colorados and kill somebody?"

Bitterness came over the muchacho's features as he turned back to Jack.

"I shoot nobody. But I would kill the gringo that killed *mi papá*, and gringos like him."

Jack drew the Bisley from his rope belt and displayed the notches. Under the high sun, the sheen of the fresh cuts was even brighter.

"So you didn't kill anybody," he challenged. "Why would you cut the frame the way you did?"

"It already that way."

Jack checked the butt and noted again Roberto's initials scratched next to the serial number, 209664.

"So where did you get it?"

Roberto wouldn't answer.

"This is twice I've seen you going or coming out of bandit country. You had a six-shooter your sister doesn't know where you got. It's got two notches that look as fresh as your initials. You've got Mary worried sick you're mixed up with the wrong kind of people."

"I shoot nobody." Roberto gigged his horse. "But if I did, it would be a gringo."

The muchacho pulled away, the distance between them growing in more ways than one.

Outside her home, Mary was stoking the fire at the cast-iron wash pot when Roberto rode up.

"Where have you been, my brother?"

She had asked the question often during the last several months, and Roberto was as tight-lipped now as before. But he looked more worn than usual, and he carried lines in his face that no fifteen year old should have as he dismounted with an exhausted sigh. When he placed a forearm across the animal's shoulder and leaned in to rest his lowered head against his wrist, Mary started toward him with concern.

"What is wrong, Roberto?"

"Nada, nothing," he said as he straightened.

Mary knew that this wasn't a time to chastise him for speaking Spanish. He proceeded to hitch the roan to the lean-to post and fold the stirrup across the seat of the saddle. She stopped at the horse's nose and watched over the suspended reins as the boy began unbuckling the cinch.

"You have ridden him hard," she said, stroking the animal's forehead. "You should brush him well."

For the first time, Roberto looked at her. "Why did you give Mister Landon my *pistola*?"

"Why do you ask that?"

"He's on his way to Candelaria with it."

"On his way—?"

"He rides a gray caballo."

The smoke from the fire had followed Mary, and suddenly it was bitter and choking.

"He is coming back?" she asked worriedly.

"Why wouldn't he come back, with you still here?"

Mary was relieved, but she was also perplexed. "What do you mean?"

"He likes you. He told me so. What were the words he used? He says you're pretty and smart. I told him you like him in the way a señorita likes a man."

"You told him that, Roberto?" she asked, embarrassed.

"It's true, isn't it?"

If dreams were an indication, it was true, all right. Every night since he had walked her home, Jack Landon had lived in her dreams, and they had stayed with her through all the weeks in which they had taught school so near to one another and yet so far apart.

"Do you disapprove, my brother?"

The cinch free, Roberto went around to the right side of the horse.

"He is a gringo," he said, throwing the cinch strap and far stirrup across the seat.

"He is a good man, Roberto."

He looked at her from across the horse's angling neck. "He was a real vaquero, Marita. He runs his caballo like a vaquero. *Madre de Dios,* he can ride!"

Unlike the day at school when Jack Landon had described the stampede, Roberto did not try to hide his excitement.

"Can he, my brother? You were riding together?"

But as Roberto returned to the roan's left side and dragged the saddle and blanket off the withers, he grew irritable again.

"Good or bad, he's still a gringo like the one who killed Papa."

His eyes glistened as he carried the saddle under the lean-to, and as soon as he laid it across a wooden trestle, he hung his head.

"I want Papa." He struggled to say the words. "All . . . All I want is Papa."

"I know, Roberto. I know you do."

He brought a hand to his face and began to sob, and it distressed Mary so much that she, too, was overcome by emotion. She went to him, and when she placed an arm around his shoulders, he turned and fell into her embrace. She could feel his shoulders shake as they stood there, a sister and brother mourning what they could never change. All the while, a dove cooed mournfully and an uncaring wind moaned through the overhead thatching that their father had laid.

In all the months since he had died, this was the first time Roberto had let Mary see him weep openly, and it broke her heart.

"He is with Mama," she whispered. "We . . . We will see him again."

"I want to see him *now*, Marita. Why did he have to die?"

Through her blouse, she could feel wetness where Roberto's face touched her shoulder, but she could only wrap him closer in her arms, for she had no answer. Nevertheless, Roberto voiced one of his own.

"He died because of gringos. I hate Jack Landon!"

Mary pulled back, her hands sliding to the boy's shoulders. "Do not say that, Roberto. Please do not say that!"

"I told him you're like a whore to him," he said angrily.

Startled, Mary couldn't find words.

"A whore!" he repeated. "That's all you are to a gringo!"

"Why would you accuse him of a thing so bad?"

Roberto broke free from her hands. "Because he is like all gringos!"

Without attending to his horse further, he stormed away, leaving Mary adrift in a gloomy world that had held such hope only moments before.

The way a señorita likes a man.

They had been the words of someone who knew Mary intimately, and as the miles dragged on during the ride back from Candelaria, Jack swayed to his horse's gait and dwelled on his place in her affections.

With every pace of the dapple gray under a furnace of a sun, Mary lived in Jack's thoughts, and for a moment, so did Annie. Mary's adobe home stood so ignoble in comparison to the white house and picket fence of Annie's dreams, and yet the difference was less stark than the disparity between the two young women. If Jack had harbored any doubt where his own affections lay, it was dispelled when he tried to summon up a memory of being with Annie, for Mary's face immediately supplanted hers.

Outside of Esperanza well into the night, he bathed at a hot spring on the river and washed his clothes. He donned them wet and rode on, guided by the melancholy strum of a guitar. It had been a long day, and he was glad when he reached his home and changed into dry apparel. His heart was set on seeing Mary, but it was late and he suspected that she was already asleep. As the guitar fell silent, he sank into a chair at the table and saw so many things in the hissing flame of the kerosene lamp.

But the only one who mattered was a comely señorita of Mexican heritage.

Jack's door was open, for the evening was hot, and he must have caught a sound or scent that led him to turn toward it. A graceful figure stood outside, aglow in the lamplight, a breeze rippling her cotton skirt.

"Mary?" he scooted back his chair and stood. "What are you doing out so late?"

"Hold me, Jack Landon."

He met her in the doorway, and she came into his arms and laid her head against his shoulder. She was shaking, and although Jack had yearned for a moment in which they might embrace again, he hadn't expected it to be like this.

But maybe his arms were the balm she needed.

For a long while, he held her just as she had asked, too concerned about her emotional state to value the dainty hands behind his shoulders or the way she yielded to his touch. But it was even better to feel needed by her, and gradually her tremble subsided.

"Three times I have come by," Mary said quietly.

"I was in Candelaria. What's wrong?"

"I worry about Roberto. I worry about you . . . and me."

Had she begun thinking of the two of them as an *us*?

Her words were so unexpected that Jack said nothing. But she had a question for him as she withdrew enough for the lamp to show in her eyes.

"What am I to you, Jack Landon?"

What could he tell her, when he didn't know the answer himself? Was she only a resting place—a *descanso*, the Mexicans called it—for a dead man searching and never finding? Or did he see in her something deeper that might assuage, if not heal, the unquenchable void inside?

"You're my friend," he managed. *My friend and more*, he wanted to add.

"Roberto said things. He told me . . . He . . ."

Through his hands on her shoulders, Jack could feel her shudder return.

"Told you what?" he asked. Then he remembered the charge that Roberto had leveled against him, and he wondered if the muchacho had shared the same accusation with her.

"Listen," he continued, "I don't know what your brother might have said, but I want you to know you've got my utmost respect."

For a moment, the lamplight burned deeper in her gaze, and then she looked away, as if mortified by embarrassment.

"I am ashamed," she said. "For you to think I would believe him, I am ashamed."

Now it was Jack who felt remorse. "I'm sorry. I shouldn't have jumped to the wrong conclusion. I . . . I'm just . . . sorry."

Sadness choked her voice. "All afternoon I have worried. The day went dark when Roberto told me what he had said to you. I worried that my brother hurt you so much that you . . ."

She faced him and went on. ". . . that you would never come back."

Surprised, he responded impulsively. "I'm not going anywhere. You can count on it."

But could she? Could she really?

They looked at one another, and as the seconds passed, Jack could see reassurance buoy the drooping lines in her face.

"You have been so good to us, Jack Landon. So good to me."

She drew nearer and kissed him on the cheek, and then she started away, only to hesitate.

"Would you sit with us when Mass is celebrated tomorrow?" she asked.

"If you'd like."

"I will meet you at ten in the courtyard."

With a smile, she vanished into the night and left Jack to ponder even more things than before.

CHAPTER 13

As the Sunday sun hung in the morning sky, Jack found Mary waiting outside the mission doors as she had promised.

In a dream that had lasted the night, the open road had vied with her embrace for all of Jack's tomorrows, and neither one had given ground. Now, as he saw her holding her plain cotton dress in place against an annoying wind, the road to nowhere seemed as far away as the house with the picket fence. Annie had never let Jack see her without cosmetics, but with the gusts sweeping aside Mary's veiling hair, he appraised a face as refreshing in its naturalness as her very character.

Mary spoke his name, and he escorted her inside with a hand on her back. Midway down the aisle, they edged in on the left beside Roberto, who, after flashing a disapproving look, scooted unnecessarily far away.

Through much of the Mass, Jack sat confused by the ritual, but when Father Diego spoke of *esperanza*, hope, he straightened and listened intently. It had not been by man's design, said the padre, that the village had been named Esperanza, for living in "Hope" had carried its people through famine and flood and pestilence. Now, said the old priest, villagers faced their greatest challenge in the guise of revolution, banditry, and wrongdoing by the very authorities charged with protecting Esperanza.

Father Diego didn't have to name names for Jack. His memory of sunburst silver dollars dropping into greedy hands was all too fresh, and so was the threat by Riggs.

113

"A day of reckoning comes for Esperanza," prophesied the padre.

Jack feared it as well, but he could do only as Father Diego urged the parishioners.

"*Por favor*, hold to hope. It is where we live."

As Jack escorted Mary toward the double doors at the close of Mass, Roberto brushed past, and he was already out of sight when they reached the courtyard.

"Roberto was anxious to leave," said Jack as they started for Mary's home. "He didn't seem pleased about you and me sitting together."

"He grieves for our father. Sometimes he sees you as a gringo like the man who killed Papa and the ones who let him go unpunished." Then her expression brightened. "But there are times when Roberto looks up to you. Yesterday he could not hide his excitement at how you rode like a vaquero."

Jack was surprised that Roberto had spoken of the incident in Mexico. To his own way of thinking, informing Mary would only upset her. It was the same reason Jack had spared her a pointless reminder of Ranger abuse by disclosing why he had gone to Candelaria.

"So what was it Roberto said?" Jack probed.

" '*Madre de Dios*, he can ride!' " she recounted with delight. "What were you and my brother doing?"

Jack didn't want to lie to her, so he avoided the question. "He's a good boy. He just needs some direction in his life."

Just as Jack did as well.

Mary grew quiet, as if deep in thought, and her silence persisted as they swung heel to toe toward her home. While they were still in sight of the yucca hill above the mission, she stopped and faced it, inducing Jack to do the same.

"The cross that watches over Esperanza is neglected," she

said, calling Jack's attention to the summit monument blazed in the sky.

Indeed, the upright section leaned and the transverse beam was awry, denying the cross its intended appearance.

"I was looking up at it when I was feeding my chickens," said Jack. "I think lightning must have hit it."

"Yes, during the storm that brought the flood. The men have been too busy with the new ditch to repair it."

"We can't let another flood happen. I'm sorry I wasn't around to help yesterday. I'll try to be down in the arroyo first thing Saturday."

Mary touched his arm. "You are so kind, Jack Landon. To help Esperanza the way you have done—you are so kind."

Jack couldn't look at her. Every time she extolled his supposed virtues, he realized again how disappointed she would be if she really knew him.

"Will you do something more for Esperanza?" she asked. "For me?"

He turned, knowing that there was nothing he wouldn't do for her.

"Would you take Roberto with you and repair our cross?" she continued.

"I better do it on my own. He's not any too keen on being around me any more than he has to be."

"It would be good for him. He has no worthy man in his life for direction. I am his sister, and I do what I can for him, but it is not enough."

Jack supposed she had a point, but he couldn't forget the look the muchacho had given him in the mission.

"My brother would want to go with you," Mary added. "A cross has always watched over Esperanza, and our father was its keeper. Through windstorms and fire from the sky, he cared for it and Roberto helped, until . . ."

For a moment, she couldn't say more, and then she found emotional words. "For his papá, Roberto would want to go."

They walked on, and when they reached the door to Mary's home, she stopped and turned.

"I am glad you are here, Jack Landon. I am glad you came back from Candelaria."

They were on display before other villagers returning from Mass, and Jack waited, wondering if he should initiate physical contact if she didn't. She drew nearer almost imperceptibly, but she seemed as uncomfortable with the lack of privacy as he was. Then their hands brushed and he took hers discreetly, and they said goodbye with a caress of fingers that made the road to nowhere seem even farther away.

Roberto seemed to struggle with his emotions as they reached the yucca hill behind the mission early the next Saturday.

Steep and banded with rimrock, it rose eighty-five feet above the bell tower and jutted to a dramatic promontory that overlooked Esperanza. With sunrise imminent, Jack and the muchacho started up through the yucca from the west side, so that they climbed into a sky growing ever brighter. From a big cottonwood the day before, Jack had sawed a ten-foot limb and a six-foot limb, and now Roberto preceded him up as they carried the larger.

Summiting, they faced a distorted X silhouetted against the sun's arc as it broke over the sawtoothed horizon. The dilapidated cross marked the point of a mesa forty yards across, and over its eighty yards of breadth grew only scattered sotol. Set below the beetling Candelaria Rim that dominated the distance from northwest to northeast, it was a lonely place that seemed fit for the kind of marker that Jack had always associated with graveyards.

They deposited the timber alongside the cross, a weathered,

eight-foot monument of unhewn cottonwood. Now that Jack stood before it, he confirmed what he had suspected from a distance: Lightning had split the vertical section down to its base, the transverse beam's loose binding alone holding it together.

"The result of the sky fire we saw from the roof the night of the flood," Jack explained. He glanced in the direction from which they had come. "We need to bring the other limb up."

He started away, but a muffled sob stopped him. Roberto stood in place, his wet cheeks gleaming in the new sun's rays.

"*Mi papá* make this," he said in English. His gaze was turned upward to the damaged cross. "I help him when I was a mucha-cho."

"I know. Your sister told me."

"Can . . . Can we make it better?"

"You mean fix it instead of replacing it?" asked Jack.

"Papa is gone. I never see him no more. Papa is gone."

As the seconds passed, Roberto's emotions chipped away at what remained of the callousness that Jack had nurtured as a reporter. He studied the splayed beam and weighed his options against a boy's need to preserve this manifestation of someone who was never coming back.

"I'll tell you what, Roberto. Run get the shovel and we'll see what we can do. Maybe we can set the new timber flush against the split one and bind it where it will hold."

Roberto soon returned and they set to work in the rocky soil, with Jack digging and the boy scooping out with his hands the loose fill that escaped the shovel blade.

"Your father meant a lot to you, didn't he," said Jack.

"Things always fun with him. Working the crops always fun with him."

"Work's good for a person. Doesn't matter if you're a man or a boy."

"I was just a muchacho. *Mi papá* would cut marks on little sticks for us. We put them down in the row and I help him open the gate. Our sticks raced in the water and I run and watched. Sometimes my stick win, sometimes Papa's. Papa tell me to make sure all crop gets water. I would go to end and do like Papa say: 'Lay down in row and take *siesta.*' When water get to me, it wake me up and I would go close the gate."

"Sounds like you had a special relationship," said Jack. "Not all fathers and sons do."

How well Jack knew it, and for a moment he wondered if his own father even realized that he had disappeared from the face of the earth.

After they dropped the new timber in place, Roberto supported it while Jack filled the excavation and tamped the soil and rocks with the end of the shovel handle. With the pole stable alongside the original, the muchacho held the crossbeam in position while Jack bound the three timbers with rawhide. He had doubted that this would work, but with a figure eight pattern, he succeeded in drawing the split sections together and bracing the existing cross with the new timber.

The restoration finished, Jack and Roberto backed away and considered their handiwork from the side that sentineled the village.

"We did a bang-up job, if I say so myself," said Jack. "I think your father would have been proud."

While Roberto had been occupied with repairs, he had kept his emotions in check. Now, though, he seemed to fight back a sob.

"*Sí*, Papa . . . Papa will watch over me from here."

And over Mary too, hoped Jack. Or, at least, he envied Roberto for being able to believe such a thing of someone as clearly special to them as their father had been.

"You know what a role model is, Roberto?" asked Jack.

"A role—?"

"It's somebody you want to be like. Anybody like that for you?"

"*Mi papá.* Only *mi papá.*"

"I thought so. Sounds like you couldn't make a better choice."

Jack allowed the exchange to sink in before asking something for which Mary had already told him the answer.

"So who all did your father like? Ever hear him say?"

"Everybody. He like everybody."

Jack had cautiously approached the matter, and now the time was right. "White people too?"

Roberto turned to him and stared, a bitter, grieving boy facing a gringo and abruptly caught in a dilemma.

"Anytime you make a choice," added Jack, "it's good to ask yourself what your papá would do in your place."

Jack didn't press the issue further and risk forcing the boy away. He had made his point, and it would be up to Roberto to make what he would of it.

Nearing Mary's door, Jack looked up at the thatched eaves and remembered the desperate moments when he had pinned her with his arm to the hard-clay roof. The howling winds had been powerful, but not so powerful as the feelings that she had stirred in him since that night. Day by day, they grew stronger, but he sensed that even she could never satisfy his inexplicable need for something that was at once like hunger or thirst, but far greater than either.

Through the open doorway, Mary must have seen him coming, for she appeared from out of the background shadows as he stopped at the threshold.

"You are finished?" she asked eagerly.

"Can you come outside? I'm on my way to help with the flood control, but I want to show you what we did first."

"How was my brother?" she asked as she stepped out.

"It was emotional for him, but I'm glad you asked me to take him along. I think it might have helped him. For one thing, I wouldn't have known how important it was to him to keep the original sections that he and your father put up."

Mary was clearly excited as she rushed with streaming hair to the street so that she could have an unobstructed view of the hill. Jack followed and watched over her shoulder as she studied the monument against the faraway Rim and crossed herself.

"*Ave Maria purísima!*" she whispered. "It is like new!"

"From here, maybe. Actually, we shored it up from behind with new timber."

She went silent, and it wasn't until Jack came abreast that he noticed that she too had begun to weep.

"*Lo siento,*" he said quietly. "I'm sorry it makes you sad, Mary."

"Yes, it makes me sad," she said, brushing her cheek. "But it also makes me happy, Jack Landon."

Turning, she hugged him, a warm, caring hug that seemed more than a gesture of appreciation, for her hands lingered on the back of his shoulders no matter who might see. When she withdrew, Jack nodded toward the monument.

"It's like a sentinel. Roberto talked like your father would watch over him from there."

"It is a nice thought," she said, checking the hill again. "At least I know Jesucristo will watch over us."

Again, Jack pondered how a cross could have come to mean so much to so many people.

"Can you help me understand something?" he asked, studying the promontory. "It's not pleasant to think about, but one time I covered a hanging for the newspaper. I can't imagine why timbers like the ones Romans impaled a prisoner on nineteen hundred years ago are any more significant than a scaffold with a noose."

"The hanged man is dead?" Mary asked.

Jack gave a half laugh. "That's a pretty safe bet, I'd say."

"Jesucristo did not stay dead. We have hope because His tomb is empty."

Jack looked at her, and continued to stare as she went on.

"I will tell you what Father Diego says. Jesucristo suffered and died for our sins, and we are healed by His stripes and the blood He poured out for us. A cross is foolishness to those who do not believe Jesucristo was raised. Do you not believe it? You *must*, Jack Landon."

He read such disillusionment in her face, disillusionment and concern, and it grieved him more than he had thought possible.

"I . . ." Jack wanted to tell her again that he wasn't who she thought he was, but he couldn't bring himself to make her even more disappointed in him.

"I enjoyed going to Mass with you," he managed.

He was appeasing, but he was also hinting, and he was glad when she smiled and touched his arm.

"I am certain Father Diego will speak of what you and Roberto have done. Please sit with us again tomorrow."

Jack went away with anticipation for the Sunday Mass, but he also went away staring up at the hill where a simple cross pricked him with so many questions about life and beyond.

CHAPTER 14

In the thin shade of the summit cross after Mass, Jack picnicked with Mary on a gray-and-red-banded *serape* while the village below lazed in the autumn sun.

The blanket's fringed corner lifted and a ripple passed through Mary's hair, but Jack could only wish that the wind was also the reason she brushed her eyes.

"Maybe coming up here wasn't a good idea," he said.

Indeed, the rolled tortillas filled with meat stew and chopped onions remained untouched, for she had wept ever since they had spread the *serape* and sat shoulder to shoulder, with Mary on Jack's right.

"You will never know Papa," she said through her emotions as she looked up at the cross. "For that, I am sorry, Jack Landon."

"He must have been a special person, from what Roberto told me."

"He was a simple and hardworking man. He looked to the saints to guide him in all things. He could not read or sign his name, but he left kindness written in the hearts of people."

"It's not everybody that can say that about their father. Me, for one."

"You cannot?"

Now Mary turned, and when he saw her concern, he wished he had kept quiet.

"I didn't mean to make this about me," he apologized.

"No, no, no. It is all right. You have told me so little about your family."

"It's probably just as well. My father's the only one living, and he and I don't see eye to eye."

She placed a hand on his arm. "That is sad. I am sorry for this too."

The cross's transverse beam eclipsed the sun, but when Jack looked up, he saw nothing but past events that could never be changed.

He shrugged. "He had his ideas for my life, and I had mine. When I was fourteen and started writing, we went in different directions. If it wasn't something you did with your hands, he considered it a waste of time. Then when my mother died last year, we didn't have the one thing that had always kept us bonded."

Mary must have read the troubled note in Jack's voice when he spoke of his mother.

"You were close to her?" she asked. "Papa has been gone for many months, and the pain is still strong. I do not know if a year is easier."

There were matters that Jack preferred keeping to himself, and his mother's death was one of them. But as he turned to Mary, he felt compelled to open up about that tragic night. Maybe it was because they had shared their own dramatic moment as dark waters had swirled and raged and crashed against whatever was in the way.

"Some things, a person never gets over," he said, looking down. "You go to sleep haunted by it, and you wake up haunted by it. I guess the way my mother died is one of those."

Watching the gusts ruffle the *serape's* fringe, Jack proceeded to tell of the stormy night at the ranch house when his father had been away at a cattleman's convention.

"She'd always been sickly, but I noticed her having a hard

time breathing. When I asked what was wrong, she said she was having tightness in her chest and down her arm. She kept getting worse, so I got her in the auto and started to the doctor."

Jack related everything: the blinding rain and merciless hail, the howl of the wind and roar of something more ominous, the out-of-control auto and the unseen arroyo with its deadly surge. He detailed his unaccountable escape from the cold, choking waters, and lastly told of recovering his mother's remains the next day.

Jack went quiet, and then Mary's hand on his arm lifted his gaze and he saw her eyes welling again.

"I grieve with you," she said.

"I should've turned back when I couldn't see the road anymore. It's something I'll have to live with the rest of my life."

"No, no, no, you are not to blame. You know you are not to blame!"

"I made the wrong decision, and my father never let me forget it. I tried telling myself I did what I had to, but all the *could haves* and *should haves* took a toll. Then I got caught up in another drowning on the job, and between it and what happened with my mother, I took a hard look at my life and didn't like what I saw. That's how I ended up here, for better or worse."

"It is better." Mary's mouth bent in a tender smile. "For me, it is better, Jack Landon."

Jack searched her eyes, and she seemed to search his in return. To his surprise, he found himself caressing her hair, the graceful tresses silky and buoyant under his touch.

"You're good for me," he said quietly. "Just knowing you is good for me."

He was about to draw near, and Mary gave him no indication that she wouldn't be receptive. Then through the window of his Model T Touring Car, he again saw Annie—insecure, distraught Annie, sensing that he was going away forever—and Jack hesitated.

Mary was special to him, so deserving of his every consideration, and as long as his insatiable search went on, he knew he couldn't take their relationship to a place where he might do the same to her as he had to Annie. Maybe it was a sign of growth on Jack's part, or maybe it was just a reflection of his same childish notion that life was supposed to mean something.

When he withdrew his hand from her hair, Mary reached across the *serape* and took up a bundle in a white cloth.

"I have brought something for you," she said.

"We haven't even touched the other food you fixed."

Mary removed the covering and extended a book titled *Biblia* with chips on the edges and a crack in the spine.

"This was Papa's," she said.

But even as Jack accepted the Bible, he resisted. "I can't take this. If it's your father's, you need to keep it."

"He would be glad to know it is with the one who repaired the cross."

"Then Roberto should have it. He was just as much a part."

"No, no, no. Papa gave my brother his own *Biblia* for First Holy Communion. Please, now this is yours."

Jack was out of reasons to refuse her gift, so he fell silent as he thumbed through the Spanish translation and found a page where the ink seemed to have bled.

"Papa could not read it," Mary added, "but every night after our mother died in childbirth, he would hold it as he slept."

Jack studied her. "You're saying she died when Roberto was born?"

Mary hung her head. "The pages are stained with Papa's tears."

Now the discolored spots took on real meaning, and Jack stared down guiltily, knowing how unworthy he was to receive something so intimate.

"It will help you understand the cross," Mary added.

But as he looked at her again, Jack wondered if there was anything that could help him understand himself.

Gaining the welcome shade of a sprawling, lightning-split cottonwood a mile upstream of Esperanza, Roberto met with censuring looks from acne-scarred Román and slender Natividad.

From where the brothers sat on deadfall at the burbling river's edge, they checked him for only a moment before scornfully returning to their afternoon amusement. Natividad drank from a dried gourd that smelled of tequila, while, on the ground before them, Román used a stick to tease an angry tarantula the size of his hand.

"How could you be so worthless, Roberto?" Román asked in Spanish without a glance.

"I'm not worthless. Did you see the cross on the hill?"

"Who cares about the cross?"

"*Mi papá* took care of it," defended Roberto. "Now I take care of it for him."

"You and the gringo teacher," interjected Natividad.

"Why you care what your papá did?" pressed Román.

"He's my role model," Roberto answered proudly.

"Your what?" asked Natividad.

"I want to be like him."

Román sneered as he raised his head. "You mean dead? Killed by a gringo?"

For a while, there was only the rustle of the cottonwood's leaves. Roberto wished that Román hadn't summoned up the terrible images—of his papá thrashing on the ground, of his blood pooling and staining, of his dilated pupils freezing in a death stare. But the pockmarked teenager had done so, and all

Roberto could do was gaze at the tarantula and feel just as tortured.

"You're worthless," Román said again. "Why don't you ever show up at Chico Cano's camp when you're supposed to?"

"When I tried last time, bandits wouldn't let me. They tried to take my caballo."

Román laughed derisively. "What bandido would want a nag like yours?"

"They put a *pistola* in my face."

"So how did you get away?" Natividad asked doubtfully.

Roberto knew better than to tell of Jack Landon's role, so he didn't reply.

"Stop making up stories," Román ordered. "You're too scared to be an hombre like Natividad and me instead of a muchacho."

"I'm not scared. They chased me and shot at me. I hugged my caballo's neck and rode hard while the bullets screamed by. Nobody ever shot at you when you rode against the store at Boquillas. You wouldn't know what it's like."

Román clearly couldn't stand the thought of Roberto passing a test of mettle that neither he nor his brother had faced. His face darkened, and when he couldn't dispute the charge, he used the stick to toss the tarantula at Roberto.

"Quit your lying, *cabrón*!" Román snarled.

Roberto caught the loathsome giant of a spider in his cheek and fell away, crying out and slapping at his face. He didn't know where the hairy thing went, or what its inch-and-a-half fangs might have done, but fear drove him to scramble away on all fours the moment he struck the ground.

"Look at him!" cried Román. "*Sí*, really brave! Run, little muchacho. Tuck your tail between your legs and run!"

Roberto was all right as he came to his feet and dusted himself off. But as he watched the tarantula crawl away, he didn't know how he would ever live down the humiliation heaped on him by the brothers, whose disdainful laughter seemed never to end.

"Go home, little muchacho!" said Román. "Los Banderos Colorados is for men, not *niños!*"

Roberto didn't want to go. These were his friends, no matter how they might treat him.

"I'm a man," he contended. "I'm nearly as old as Natividad."

"Then prove it, little muchacho. Chico Cano will ride against a gringo ranch when the time is right. He wants hombres, not *niños.* You man enough to ride with us?"

Roberto hesitated. "Why does Cano pick a gringo ranch to ride against?"

"Gringos took everything from us," spoke up Natividad. "Cano takes back what's ours."

"They're sons of El Diablo, the devil," said Román. "Every gringo's the same."

Roberto had heard it all before, and had even repeated it, but now he listened with the ears of his father. "*Mi papá* liked everybody. He—"

"A gringo killed him," interrupted Román. "Other gringos turned that gringo loose so he could kill some other Mexicano. You think your papá would like them?"

Roberto didn't have an answer, or maybe he did. His papá had been a forgiving man who, if his death hadn't been so sudden, might have followed the examples of Jesucristo and Saint Stephen and prayed that the gringo be absolved of his murder.

Roberto was still dwelling on it when Román stood and looked down on him.

"Go home, little muchacho!" Román said again with a wave of his arm. "You ever decide to be a man, find your *pistola* and prove it when Cano rides against a gringo ranch."

CHAPTER 15

As the months passed at school, Jack noticed a change coming over Roberto.

Before, the muchacho had participated only grudgingly, speaking only in answer to direct questions. Because of his clear aversion to attending, his learning had been stifled, even as Jack had continued to believe in his potential. He was, after all, Mary's brother.

Now, though, Roberto seemed to be developing a real interest, and his native intelligence began setting him apart from Jack's other students. His retention of information was impressive, and Jack also saw signs of analytical skills and abstract reasoning. As Roberto climbed step by step out of a pit of grief and bitterness, he was proving what Jack knew all too well: Emotional matters could not only impact a person, but cripple him, and only by overcoming could he achieve his utmost.

On this Friday afternoon in mid-December, Roberto was particularly engaged when it came his turn to read aloud from a story. Jack had been displeased with the selections in the school reader, for there was little in their subject matter to interest someone in Esperanza. He solved the issue by crafting a story of his own and not only setting it in the village, but including as characters all of his students. Indeed, a different pupil starred in each new chapter.

Except for his missives to the adjutant general's office and *El Paso Morning Times,* it was the first substantive writing Jack had done since the *San Angelo Daily Standard*. Finally free of the impossibly high standards he had set for himself, he enjoyed the process for the first time in years. Furthermore, he had never witnessed the impact of his work on a reader, so it was rewarding to see the pleasure in the young faces as he handed out copies of the chapter titled "Roberto and the Little Burro."

Jack's goal was threefold: to promote reading comprehension, teach proper grammar, and instill values at a critical time in his students' lives. In the way of principles, his story stressed the importance of choosing right over wrong, being true to worthy friends, lending a helping hand, and showing respect for the *viejos* and *viejas,* the village elders. For too many years, Jack had written for the wrong reasons; maybe now he had discovered the kind of writing he was born to do.

Mary typically kept the younger students focused on their own tasks, but she had been so impressed by Jack's approach that today, as every day this week, she allowed them to listen. From where Jack stood facing the classroom, he could see her smiling from a back bench to the right of the door, while in front of her, the eager children leaned forward and cupped chins in hands in rapt attention.

As Roberto read aloud and the older students followed along on their copies, he stumbled over many words but took obvious pride in navigating every sentence. Even in his struggles, there was delight in his face as he narrated his fictional self's rescue of the orphan foal of a wild burro. His misadventures in trying to get a nanny goat to adopt the little burro were the things of comedy, and Roberto was laughing louder than anyone when the door burst open and a dark figure appeared against the outside brightness and entered.

"School's done with," a gruff voice announced.

Roberto turned with everyone else, leaving the jingle of spurs the only sound. As the featureless shadow moved away from the blinding background, Jack recognized someone he had hoped never to see again. From the rawboned build to the tangle of red whiskers that dripped with tobacco juice, the ranger named Riggs was all too familiar. He had his .45 six-shooter out, and he carried it, muzzle down, along his thigh as he stopped a few steps inside the door and scanned the classroom.

"Little pepper bellies and—hey, whadda we got here?" Riggs looked Mary up and down. "Damn, if you ain't—"

Jack didn't let him finish. "Excuse me, we're in the middle of class."

Riggs scowled at him. "Told you school's over."

An unpleasant drama was unfolding, and the tension was building by the moment. Jack could hear it in the ranger's voice and see it in Mary's features, and he didn't know what to do except get her and the children out as quickly as possible and limit the confrontation to one against one.

"Miss Contreras," said Jack, addressing Mary, "why don't we go ahead and let school out early."

Few students ever had to be told twice to go home after school, and as the pupils responded, Mary went to the door and ushered them out with a repeated "Hurry, children. You must hurry." Roberto alone seemed to realize that trouble brewed, and he paused at the threshold and faced his sister.

"It is all right, Roberto," she said. And then she forced a smile and added, as if to relieve his worry, "I want to hear more about the little burro tomorrow."

With a concerned glance back at Riggs, Roberto went on outside, and when Mary didn't follow immediately, Jack drew her attention.

"You go on home, Miss Contreras. I'll be leaving soon."

Before she could act, Riggs took her arm. "Hold on here, señorita. I think you better stay."

Jack stepped forward. "Turn her loose—what do you think

you're doing?"

With his boot, the ranger closed the door, leaving only the open windows to provide light. His grip on Mary's arm stayed firm, and he twisted her around to a bench on the right.

"Sit yourself down. I got business with this Meskin lover here."

Forced to comply, Mary sat, and even though she may have never seen Riggs before, Jack knew that she probably surmised plenty from the *cinco peso* badge on his soiled woolen shirt.

Jack was only an arm's length away now, but he got no closer, for he abruptly saw Riggs over the dark muzzle of the ranger's .45 Colt.

Riggs's cheek developed a tic. "First person I see when I ride into town, I ask him, 'Say, that white boy livin' here, all dressed up Meskin. Speaks it good too. Know where I can find him?' Teaches school, the old wetback tells me, and what do you know? Meskin lover's right here where he says, teachin' little greasers that ain't got snot for brains."

"What do you want?" asked Jack.

Riggs dug into his shirt pocket and brought out a folded piece of yellowing paper. It rustled as he opened it with one hand and shook it in Jack's face. The masthead said *El Paso Morning Times,* and spread across two columns in the lower right corner was a headline circled in pencil: "Who Are the Real Bandits"?

"What in hell you know about this?" Riggs grunted.

This wasn't the time for bravado. Jack scanned the months-old article, finding it word for word as he had written it, without identifying names or locations other than "a border town."

"Byline says 'Border Correspondent,' " said Jack.

"That's you, ain't it?"

"Why would you think that?"

Riggs stuffed the clipping back in his shirt and spat a stream of tobacco juice that caught Jack in the bend of his elbow. "Maybe them other boys in B Company's cowed by you, but I ain't one of 'em."

Jack glanced at his stained sleeve. "I don't imagine Esperanza's the only place you go. So why—"

"Nobody else got smarts enough to write letters. Or maybe it wasn't so smart of you after all."

With a menacing double click, Riggs cocked the .45. "Warned you, you bastard," the ranger growled, "you don't cross me."

Jack's heart pounded, and suddenly he couldn't find a breath. "Shooting somebody white . . ." He thought of Mary's father. "The courts won't let somebody off as easy."

"Captain Fox has got our backs. Soon's I finish with you, I'm collectin' for him from that Meskin priest you got." He gave Mary a quick look again. "But first I'm gonna do some collectin' of my own."

Jack didn't know what to do.

He saw the black muzzle and the edge-on fin of the sight. He saw the cylinder under the barrel, four bays rammed tight with .45 cartridges. He saw a bristly jaw knotted with tobacco, and wide, wild orbs as bloodshot as a streaked sky at a dying sun. But most of all, Jack saw Mary—virtuous, blameless Mary— and she watched in fear as she gripped the edge of the bench.

"Your . . . Your problem's with me, not with her," Jack managed. "Let her leave."

"Now why the hell would I do what *you* want?"

When Riggs had trained his revolver on him back in the courtyard, Jack hadn't really believed that he would shoot. This time, Jack felt no such assurance; the darting pupils of the bulging eyes were just too crazy.

But Jack could only crumple to searing pain in his chest— fitting payback for a life largely squandered in self-interest— while selfless, caring Mary would endure a hell certain to haunt her the rest of her life.

"You will leave here at once!"

Abruptly Mary was up, defiant against Riggs and his .45, and as much as Jack had admired her already, he held her in higher regard now.

The ranger turned. "Spitfire, ain't you? I'll settle you down, you—!"

Jack lunged for the revolver.

He struck it under the barrel and drove the muzzle upward. The six-shooter roared over his shoulder and he flinched to stinging fire. Simultaneously Riggs whirled with an oath, and suddenly the two of them were grappling with a .45 primed to kill. Jack could taste the bitter gun smoke and feel the hot barrel as the sight gouged his palm, and the struggle didn't end until the ranger wrenched the weapon free and the barrel flashed down in a punishing blow above Jack's eye.

The world went dark.

It stayed that way as the floor surged up with grim force, and then out of a quick sunburst of dancing specks, he saw Mary wade into the fight. An instant later the barrel whipped down again, and this time a lasting dark fell and lay across Jack like coins over a dead man's eyes.

When the school door slammed shut and confined Mary with the gringo ranger, Roberto feared the worst.

He could have lingered outside at the threshold, or peered through a side window, but nothing about this felt right and he turned one way and then another, helpless and yet frantic with an urgency to give succor.

"You ever decide to be a man, find your *pistola.*"

They had been Román's goading words under the cottonwood, and as Roberto had listened with the ears of his role model, he had dismissed them. But his papá would have protected Mary at all costs, and as Roberto realized it, he bolted along the face of the school for Jack Landon's attached home.

Alarmed chickens scattered with squawks and a flurry of down as he broke around the corner and raced to the closed door. Locks were unknown in Esperanza, and the muchacho burst inside and spun left and right. He rummaged through papers on the table and dug into a battered chest, and when that proved fruitless, he scoured the rock shelf over the fireplace and flung aside the kindling in the corner. Next he combed a side room and hurried into another, finding a cast-iron bedstead with cotton garments dangling from the rusted post at its head.

He stripped the bed covers down to the broken springs and was almost ready to give up until he brushed the hanging garments and felt something hard. Tossing the clothes aside, he found a cracked chamois pouch suspended by its drawstring, and he grabbed it and rushed outside. Withdrawing the Bisley and a fistful of .38-.40 cartridges, he loaded the six-shooter as he ran again through the frightened chickens and negotiated the corner.

He reached the school door and found it closed as before. The other students had dispersed, leaving the playground empty except for Roberto's roan and an unfamiliar chestnut horse hitched to a lone mesquite. A piercing gunshot spurred the muchacho on around the far corner, and he came up before an open window and threw his back up against a mud-brick wall baking in the sun. Sliding down into a crouch, he proceeded to rise little by little until he could peer around the jamb.

He saw the ranger pistol-whipping Jack Landon, and Mary closing with the hombre to stop it. He saw the mad-dog look as the *bastardo* wheeled and backhanded her in the face. He saw Mary's hair fly as she fell back, crashing over a bench and overturning it. And just as he had witnessed their father's murder, Roberto saw her look up so vulnerably at her assailant as the white devil advanced with a motive that was all too clear.

Roberto cocked the Bisley and fired.

The ranger's gun arm jerked as the blast rocked the schoolroom. The .45 spilled from the gringo's fingers and he looked up, clutching his forearm. For a moment the muchacho faced him over the smoking barrel of the Bisley, and then Roberto cocked and fired again, chasing the ranger out the door.

Roberto pursued as far as the corner, where he watched the frantic gringo free the chestnut from the mesquite and awkwardly swing astride. Keeping his bloody arm across his *cinco peso* badge, the ranger looked back, making brief eye contact a second time, and spurred the animal away.

Roberto assured himself that the man wasn't returning and then rushed back to the window. Boosting himself up on the sill, the muchacho climbed through, his sister's name on his lips. She seemed dazed as she tried to drag herself up by means of the overturned bench, but when Roberto reached her and said her name again, she turned and her eyes were now clear.

But there was nothing that could erase so easily the welt on her cheek.

"The *bastardo* hit you, Marita!" he said in Spanish.

"See about Jack Landon, my brother. Quickly!"

On the floor in the aisle, the teacher squirmed and moaned. He was shaking his head as well, slinging droplets of blood from cuts in his brow, but Roberto gave him only a glance.

"Jack Landon's a gringo!" he said. "He's a devil like all the others!"

Roberto broke for the door, the Bisley Model Colt fierce in his hand as he had more to say.

"I'll kill the gringo ranger!"

"No, Roberto! No!"

But the muchacho was already outside, ruled again by a white man's murder of their father.

Jack Landon! Jack Landon!

Carried on a disembodied voice, the name seemed to come up out of a deep well and play in the recesses of Jack's mind. He knew that he should respond, but a nightmare had him in its grip, and the part of him that turned thought into speech was numbed.

Strange, the sensations that spoke to him in this moment— the brush of buoyant hair on his cheek, the specks of light winking against a moving shadow, the scent of a freshly sharpened lead pencil, the metallic, even rusty, taste of blood on his lips. And that incessant voice that called his name.

Jack awoke, alert but half blinded by sweat in his eyes. Mary's face was distorted as she bent close, and he wiped his brow and saw that it was blood and not perspiration that had collected on his fingers.

"Tell me you are all right! Please tell me, Jack Landon!"

Jack sat up, his head aching and the room swimming as he remembered how she had fought to stay the whipping pistol even as she had been under the greater threat. Stricken by fear, he reached for her.

"Did he hurt you?" He ran his thumb across the welt on her cheek. "Did he do anything else?"

"No, no, no! I am all right!"

There was a tremor in her voice, and it panicked him even more until he realized that it was because he shook her by the shoulders. Relaxing his hold, he tried to read the truth in her expression.

"You're sure he—"

"Roberto did not let him. From the window, he shot him in the arm and chased him away."

"Roberto?" Jack quickly scanned the room. "Where—"

"He left on his horse. He said he would kill the man of the *cinco peso*. I . . . I am afraid for my brother."

"He did the right thing, shooting him. But he can't take it any farther."

Mere words couldn't console her, and Jack drew her close, forgetting that his touch stained her clothes. He was surprised when she withdrew with a little cry of alarm.

"There is blood! You were shot!"

Checking above his shoulder, Jack found a bloody tear in white cotton darkened by powder residue.

"Creased me is all, I think." Riggs's six-shooter lay nearby, and he seized it and counted five cartridges still unspent. "Roberto—I've got to go after him."

With Mary's help, he struggled to his feet, but he had to hold to her arm when the floor seemed to rise and fall.

"How can you do this?" she asked.

"Just help me to the horse Longino Castaneda keeps for me."

Minutes later, from the stirrups of the dapple gray, Jack looked down at Mary's upturned face.

"Once I ride off," he said, "you've got to clean up the blood in the schoolroom and make sure nobody says anything. I guess I never should've reported what happened outside of the mission that day."

"Listen to me, Jack Landon."

Jack listened.

"For you to know what is right—and not to do it—would grieve Jesucristo, as the blessed servant James has written. You did as God would have you do, and what comes after is by His will. More than ever, I am proud of what you have done for Esperanza. And for me."

Impulsively, Jack leaned off the side of his horse and drew

her close with a hand to the back of her head. The angle was awkward and the situation not as he would have written, but before he rode away he found her lips with his.

And there was nothing in her response to suggest that he offended her.

CHAPTER 16

From the look of the horse tracks up the Rio Grande, the two animals had been in hell-bent flight.

As Jack clung to the trail past cane and black willows on the river side and pitaya and lechuguilla in the rocky bluffs on the other, he faced a dilemma for which there seemed no solution. A boy of Mexican heritage had shot a Texas Ranger, and no matter the justification, he would be guilty of attempted murder. Even if Company B didn't string up Roberto from the nearest cottonwood, he would grow old in the state penitentiary while Riggs would reap a commendation and return to finish what he had started with Mary.

Furthermore, Jack wouldn't be around to protect her. He would face charges of aggravated assault, and he knew from his newspaper work that the courts invariably sided with a peace officer in these circumstances.

By trying to do the right thing, Jack had entangled people he cared about in an unwinnable situation. He wished he could believe as Mary did: that any consequence of a just act happens only by the will of a Higher Power who works all things together for good. Jack had spent many hours in the tear-stained pages of her father's Bible, and just a night or two ago he had read a passage to that effect. If he could ever accept the notion, it might give him a measure of the peace he needed in so many ways.

But Jack couldn't live a lie, and his agnosticism argued that he alone was responsible for finding a way out for everyone.

He reached a large, sunlit canyon where the river rushed between tiered folds of mountains bare of vegetation except sotol and sacahuista but studded with boulders. As the hoofbeats counted out the dapple gray's progress up a daunting climb that left white-capped rapids receding beneath his stirrup, a single option kept rearing its ugly head, and Jack fought against it as strongly as he did the idea of a divine plan in play.

If Riggs wasn't around to report the shooting, there could be no reckoning for Roberto. There would be no charges of aggravated assault, and most importantly, Mary would never have to look over her shoulder in the fear that she would find the ranger there.

If any man deserved to die, it was Riggs. The world would be better, and the immediate benefactors would include not only the three of them, but Señora Ramos and Father Diego and everyone else in Esperanza.

But killing a man . . .

If it came down to staring at Riggs over the cocked hammer of the ranger's own .45 and violating the most basic principle of humanity, Jack didn't know if he would have what it took.

The pitch of the climb was such that the narrow trail disappeared only forty feet above—a thread of white pointing into blue sky—and the dapple gray began to struggle. Jack could feel the hoofs slipping and hear the rubble as it rolled off what was now a sheer cliff, and more than once the animal seemed ready to drop to its knees. With nothing but an updraft to keep a rider from plunging to the murmuring rapids hundreds of feet below, this was no place for a horse to lose its footing.

After hard minutes, Jack topped out on the first of two high points a hundred yards apart across a deep saddle. Over the last ninety seconds, the dapple gray's stride had faltered, and Jack recognized the limp and the dipping nose as signs of forequarter distress. But he had greater worries as he saw the ongoing trail from this lofty vista. Down and away, Roberto, on his roan, pushed on with abandon, blind to a sudden dazzle of light beyond him on the farther rise. Jack surmised it was a rifle, for Riggs was there too, twisting around on a chestnut horse. Jack didn't know why he hadn't remembered that Riggs carried a carbine in a saddle scabbard under his leg, but there it was, reflecting the rays as he waited for the muchacho to come into sight.

Or maybe the boy already had, for with one arm the ranger awkwardly shouldered the weapon.

"Look out!" yelled Jack.

Roberto spun, shifting enough for Riggs's rifle shot to go wide. But as gravel kicked up behind the muchacho and the blast reverberated, it was the ranger who paid the price. His spooked horse went wild, catching the man off balance as it bucked.

Suddenly Riggs was tumbling down the chestnut's left hindquarter, a desperate man flailing at the edge of a cliff. The carbine struck muzzle first and went over, brilliant as it fell through the sunlight. Riggs followed with the most terrible of screams, an awful thing to hear even from one unfit to live. For an instant his boot hung to the stirrup, teasing him as he dangled over the brink, and the next moment he was gone.

The shrieks echoed and grew fainter and fainter, and then there was nothing but the taunting moan of the wind and whisper of rapids.

"*Madre de Dios!*" exclaimed Roberto.

But Jack was focused on the canyon depths and the facedown body that surged downstream, disappearing and reappearing as it rode the wicked currents. Stunned, he watched until the body went under and never came back up, even as Jack searched with his gaze as far downriver as the canyon's lower tier allowed him.

Roberto began to shout, drawing Jack's attention. The mucha-cho brandished his six-shooter as he stared over the cliff and hurled taunts at someone who could no longer hear, and as much as Jack had wanted to see Riggs dead, he hated to see Mary's brother rejoice in even a bad man's death. Not only that, but the writer in Jack took it as an ill omen when a buz-zard soared into view beyond the boy and its wheeling course carried it across the face of the sun.

"We'll never find his body, but somebody else is liable to!"

At Jack's shout, Roberto turned.

"If they do," Jack continued, "they'll see he was shot and go looking for somebody to blame!" He checked the far rise and saw the chestnut standing like a sentinel. "We can't let his horse go back in on his own. Grab him and bring him. We'll figure something out!"

Expecting Roberto to comply, Jack drew Riggs's .45 from the inside of his rope belt and threw it toward the white-capped waters below. He knew he couldn't risk keeping the weapon.

"Go to hell!"

Jack looked up at the muchacho's cry in Spanish.

"I'm through with you gringos!" the boy continued to yell at Jack. "You killed *mi papá* and hurt Marita!"

Taken aback, Jack blurted a response from the heart. "You know I'd never hurt your sister, Roberto. I love her!"

He didn't have time to digest what he had heard himself say, for the muchacho shouted back.

"I'll kill all the gringos!"

Roberto turned and pressed his horse up the pitch, and even though Jack called after him until the boy disappeared over the far rise with the ranger's chestnut, the muchacho never looked back.

And all Jack could do from the stirrups of a lame horse was watch.

When Jack told Mary what had happened to Riggs, she seemed saddened rather than relieved.

"I will pray for his soul."

They faced one another in the Saturday morning sunlight that beamed through her door, and as he gently brushed the hair from her cheek to find swelling and an ugly bruise, he was amazed that she could muster such benevolence.

"How do you do it?" he asked. "Somebody that treated you that way—how could you care?"

"I will get water and clean the dried blood on your face. It is not as easy to forgive the man of the *cinco peso* for hurting one I care about."

Care about.

It was the first time Mary had said anything like that, and as she started away, Jack remembered what he had impulsively uttered to Roberto the day before. For the rest of that long Friday, and deep into the night, Jack had replayed the moment as he had walked the trail toward Esperanza and led his crippled horse. When he had still been far from the village, the three words had stayed with him as he had unsaddled the dapple gray and sunk exhausted to the rubbly trace, the only place free of lechuguilla. There, stretched out with his head against the saddle's back housing, he had looked up and seen Mary in the thousands of stars jeweling the black sky.

And none of them had shone as brightly as she.

But with the golden memory came a dark one, and when Mary returned and set about cleaning his caked blood, he knew he had to tell her.

"I'm afraid Roberto won't ever come back as long as I'm around you."

144

Mary withdrew a little. "Not come—?"

"He seemed to be working through everything, and then this had to happen. He said gringos like me killed your father and hit you, and that he was through with us."

"You would never do such a thing, Jack Landon!"

"I tried to tell him that. I told him there's no way I'd ever hurt you, because I—"

This time, Jack caught himself before he blurted the words. How could he tell her when he hadn't even processed what was inside him?

Mary's chin quivered. "First, Papa . . . Roberto *has* to come back!"

"I know you raised him. I know what he means to you. Maybe . . . Maybe I should leave."

She began to weep. "Do not say that. Please do not say that!"

"I—"

The words didn't come easily, and Jack heard them as if they were spoken by someone else.

"If I'm out of the picture, he'll hear about it and maybe he'll come home. I know Roberto's all you've got."

There had been pain in her features, but was that hurt that he saw now?

Whatever it was, she turned away and hid it from him, and he reached for her, only to let his hand linger over her shoulder without ever touching.

"You would leave?" she pressed quietly through the emotion. "You would leave . . . the children?"

Hers may not have been the question for which Jack would have wished, but maybe it was better this way.

CHAPTER 17

It was not a pleasant thing to consider, this notion of running away again.

For the moment, at least, Jack chose to remain in Esperanza and let the option fester. Nevertheless, he kept his distance from Mary, to the extent possible, so that he might come to grips with what his intellect, and not his heart, was saying about the self-sacrifice that might bring her brother back. It was true that she had identified Jack as one she cared about, but her follow-up remarks may have already told him everything he needed to know.

She hadn't asked him to stay for her, only for the children.

For the first time in months, Jack didn't meet her for Mass. But Mary's graceful profile seemed to go with him nonetheless up the slope of the sentinel hill to the toll of the mission bell. There, under the wind-buffeted cross, he sat reading her father's Bible in the very spot where the two of them had sat. For months, she had buoyed him, carrying him to a place so lofty that Jack had forgotten what despair was like. Now that he knew again, the misery was crushing.

School on the following day was even more trying. Confined to the same room, and obligated to communicate and yet not really speak, they were together and yet farther apart than ever, and all Jack could do was count off the hours and mumble his way through the lessons. It wasn't fair to his students, and when they begged to read more of "Ricardo and the Little Burro," he was abrupt, even rude, in his refusal.

The week seemed destined to go on that way, wretched hours of turmoil that would accomplish nothing. Jack's melancholy persisted into the Wednesday before Christmastide, a morning that found him at the flood control project as the sun rose fiery through dust that billowed from a Fresno Scraper pulled by four mules abreast. The new ditch was nearing completion, and the focus was now on deepening the arroyo and constructing an embankment on the village side.

Both days after school, Jack had searched for Román and Natividad, the teenagers whom Mary had mentioned as unsavory influences on Roberto. Now he hoped to find them before classes commenced. As Jack walked up the bed of the arroyo, his sandals leaving tracks in the freshly turned dirt, he found the brothers on the far bank. Although he had never spoken with either, he knew them by reputation as well as by sight, so he was surprised to find them out at this hour where work was to be done.

Not that they were doing any. Reeking of tequila, they sat facing the rising sun, and judging from their appearance, it was clear that the brothers weren't so much up early today as still out late from the night before. Their shoulders sagged and their eyelids drooped, but they nevertheless found enough energy to puff on cigarettes and pass a dried gourd.

"When did you see Roberto last?" Jack asked.

The younger muchacho, Natividad, squinted down at Jack and mumbled something incoherent. His older brother, the intoxication flush across his face no less deep, at least was still capable of speech.

"Ahh, the gringo teacher," Román said with slurred words. "You around Marita all time, eh? Ahh, she's sweet. Tell her come see Román, eh?"

Jack had no patience for remarks about Mary.

"Roberto—have you seen him?" he repeated.

"Why you look for the worthless *pendejo*?"

"He needs to know something."

"He never be a man like us." Román looked over and elbowed his brother. "His tail between his legs—eh, Natividad? Run, brave little muchacho!"

Maybe the younger brother was beyond speech, but he could still join Román in snickering at some shared memory.

"He might've gone across the river," said Jack. "I don't know for sure. You see him, let him know I'm not around his sister anymore. I'll leave Esperanza if that's what it takes, but she wants him to come back."

Román took a swig from the gourd, and his tongue loosened. "She Mexicano like me. You need to stay away from our señoritas. You gringos take everything. We get scraps like dogs. Ahh, Christmas Day, you wait."

"What about Christmas?"

"Maybe Roberto will ride with us. Maybe by then he—"

Abruptly, Román seemed to realize he had said too much. His jaw went slack and his bloodshot eyes sobered.

"What about Christmas, Román?" Jack asked again.

Still the teenager gave no answer, and Jack stepped closer and studied his features against the sky's blue background.

"Román, are you riding with bandits?" he pressed. "That what you're planning to do? Roberto too?"

Román tugged on Natividad's arm. "*¡Vaya con prisa!*" he urged him.

Román had difficulty standing, but without his help, Natividad would never have managed. Even so, the younger brother was like an animal with the blind staggers as they started away.

Jack climbed the arroyo bank after them. "Where this time? Another place like Glenn Springs? Boquillas? You answer me, Román!"

Román looked back and waved him away. "Go to hell, gringo! I tell you nothing!"

Jack continued to call, but the brothers only stumbled on with Roberto's future hanging in the balance.

"I won't be in. Please cover for me."

After stopping by the empty school and leaving a note for Mary, Jack did the responsible thing and struck out downriver on a borrowed horse. In the afternoon, he rode into the U.S. Army camp on an elevated flat that overlooked the adobes of Candelaria and the floodplain fields on both sides of the river.

The Eighth Cavalry post consisted of two parallel rows of conical tents, with six tents to the side and a long, brush arbor down the middle so that each tent opened to the shelter. After dismounting and hitching the roan, Jack stepped under the open end of the breezy arbor and was challenged in the shade by a private in a wool campaign hat, khakis, and tight-fitting canvas leggings that came up almost to his knees. When Jack asked for the Corps of Intelligence Police, the soldier led him past a series of support poles to a table cluttered with rustling papers weighted with rocks against a wind that flapped the adjacent tents.

Behind the table sat a graying, pencil-necked captain with a pipe in his mouth, and after the introductions, Jack got right to the point.

"I have reason to believe that bandits will launch a raid on an American interest, or interests, on Christmas Day. That's all the information I have, but I urge you to alert settlements and ranches near the border."

"Where did you say you're from?"

Jack hadn't said, and he didn't intend to. He remembered Mary's concern that Esperanza's loyalties were already under suspicion, and he wasn't about to add fuel to the fire.

"I'm a freelance journalist. I've come in contact with parties up and down the river. In a drunken stupor, one of them let it slip. He didn't say where it would happen, but he specifically said it would be Christmas Day."

The captain shook his head. "Some drunk Mexican spouting off's not actionable intelligence."

"I'm just reporting what I heard this morning. Maybe there's something to it, and maybe there's not. But if I had the Army's resources, I'd make sure every American interest below the Southern Pacific knows to be vigilant at Christmas."

"So exactly where *was* this drunk you talked with? Some of these villages are full of collaborators. They're for Carranza or Villa or anybody except white Americans. They're like a den of snakes."

"He wasn't in a village. I came across him under a cottonwood on the river."

"Close to where?"

The officer was persistent, just as Jack had been with interviewees who hadn't seemed forthright.

"It wasn't near anywhere," Jack replied.

"What was the next place you came to?"

"I don't know for sure. Those villages are all so similar—adobes and fields and the like. It was just someplace up the river from here."

"How far?"

"I can't say. I've ridden a lot of river in the days since."

"I thought you said it was this morning."

Jack had fallen for an interview trick that he himself had used at times—ply a secretive subject with questions until he contradicts himself, and then challenge him on it.

The captain challenged him. Removing his pipe, the officer scooted back his chair and stood, his gray eyes piercing.

"I think you know more than you're letting on."

"Listen," said Jack. "I think there's going to be an attack six days from now, and people are liable to be killed. If I knew more about it, I'd tell you. Enough blood's been spilled on the border already."

Maybe Jack's sincerity showed through, for the captain's tight-set jaw relaxed a little.

"Yeah, fished a body out of the Rio Grande this week. Ranger badge. Looked like he'd been shot. Didn't look like a mortal wound, but he's dead just the same."

Jack hoped the officer didn't notice him shudder.

"It's a dangerous place to be, this country," said Jack. "I hope it's not worse this Christmas."

Chapter 18

To the barking of dogs, the mission bell tolled, and tolled again, in a way it hadn't since the morning after the flood.

From where she stood over a boy's shoulder to help him with his arithmetic, Mary looked through the open school window and saw villagers making their way toward the hidden mission. Between scheduled Masses, Father Diego would not bring together the people of Esperanza except for something very important, and by the babel of young voices around her, she knew that even her students were aware of it.

The ominous summons heightened the tension on an already dark Friday morning for Mary, for Jack Landon had not shown up at school again.

"I know Roberto's all you've got."

For six days now, Jack Landon had been distant, but not so distant that his words no longer dominated her waking thoughts and unsettling dreams. They had been blunt, uncompromising words that had told her that she had no place in his life. The realization had preyed on her like a lingering death, but at least she had seen him across the classroom, the two of them together even if they had been apart. Now, though, he may have done as he had proposed and left forever.

Forever.

It was too crushing to consider, and not just for her, but for his students and all of Esperanza. She hadn't known how to interpret his note from Wednesday, and when she had called his name outside his door that evening, and again on Thursday, he hadn't responded. Upon his failure to report again today, she had sent a boy to check his welfare, and when the pupil had returned alone, a great weakness had come over Mary. She had set his students to studying their textbooks in the hope that he would still arrive, but now the incessant toll of the bell seized everyone's attention.

"Children," she announced, "If you will line up, we will go to the mission."

She had to chastise them about their disorderly rush out the door, but soon she had them bunched behind her as she led the way toward the gathering crowd. Passing the last concealing adobe, she burst upon the plaza that fronted the courtyard and saw all the *viejas* and *viejos*, waiting wizened and bent; the white-clad men, squinting under the brims of floppy sombreros; and the babies, sleeping in the arms of mothers with rebosas. Almost all of Esperanza was there, exchanging confused glances as the bell in the mission tower tilted one way and then another, pealing to the strike of its clapper.

Just outside the courtyard, alongside their respective horses, stood six white men in assorted western garb, even their Stetson hats and pointed boots varying in style and degree of wear. Some of the men had their duck pants stuffed inside their boot uppers, while others had one trouser leg hitched up and the other one smoothly in place down to the heel. Two men wore suspenders against their woolen shirts, and four did not, their waists showing belts of rope or scuffed leather. The only unifying element among the six was a *cinco peso* badge that mirrored the sun as they faced the concerned townspeople.

Texas Rangers!

Mary shuddered, for she knew why they were here.

She held the children behind a group of sweaty laborers fresh from the fields and watched through the adjacent arch as the mission doors swung open. As the bell reverberated to a final toll, Father Diego appeared, looking older than ever. From the background shadows, a seventh ranger emerged and passed the lingering padre.

As the stranger crossed the courtyard toward her, Mary noted the unusual way he kept his head cocked, as if he had a spasm in his neck, and when he came through the arch and turned along the waist-high wall, she saw his flaring nostrils and tight mouth. He clearly was angry, and he was none too gentle as he pushed his way through the townspeople in order to join the other lawmen.

Mary lost sight of him, but he reappeared from the stirrups of a big bay. Reining the horse about, he faced the crowd from an elevated position that allowed all but the smallest children to see.

"I'm Wolfe, sergeant in Ranger Company B," he announced. "Everybody savvy?"

"They *better* savvy," snapped another ranger.

Wolfe went on. "One of our men's been killed. Found him in the Rio Grande near Candelaria. From the looks, he'd floated all the way from up here somewhere."

Wolfe paused and scanned left and right.

"One of you greasers shot him and throwed him in the river. Either somebody talks, or there'll be hell to pay."

Mary had expected repercussions, but even with the laborers ahead as buffers, she shrank and threw her arms out at her sides, instinctively protecting the children behind her.

"*Señores. Por favor.*"

By way of the graveyard, Father Diego had approached the rangers, and now he stood across the crumbling wall from the men.

"Why do you come to Esperanza and not another village?" he asked with wavering voice.

To a creak of leather, Wolfe twisted in the saddle and faced him.

"Damned nest of bandits, this place is. You people ain't fooling nobody."

"But, señor—"

"Went by the name of Riggs. *You* ought to remember him. Rawboned. Mid-thirties. Red whiskers. He come across a old story in the El Paso paper, 'Rangers the Real Bandits,' wrote up just like that white—" Wolfe spun to the crowd for a moment. "Where is he? The lying bastard that said he'd report us?"

"*Por favor*, please go," said the padre.

"Riggs come down to pick a bone with him and ended up dead," Wolfe told the priest. He straightened in the saddle and his voice rose, rolling like dire thunder across the townspeople.

"Who was it killed him? Somebody start talking or we're setting fire to the church!"

His words cut through Mary like the cold steel of a knife, and from all around her came audible gasps. She looked from one villager to another, seeing the ashen faces of innocent, hardworking people whose spiritual lives centered around the mission. No one had witnessed the shooting at school, but every student had seen the ranger enter, and while gunshots weren't unknown in Esperanza, a bloody man fleeing on horseback with riders in pursuit had not gone unnoticed by townspeople. Mary had urged witnesses to keep quiet about the matter, but who among them could stay silent now?

"Last chance!" warned Wolfe.

"*Por favor*, you cannot do this!" pleaded Father Diego.

Wolfe looked back at a ranger at the bay's hindquarter. He was a string bean of a man with discolored buckteeth and a crooked nose. "Do it!"

Passing the reins of his Appaloosa to Wolfe, the buck-toothed ranger climbed over the unstable stone wall, collapsing more of it, and made a show of withdrawing a match from his pocket as he started across the graveyard. As he passed Father Diego, the old padre grabbed his arm.

"*Por favor,* I beg you!"

But the ranger wrenched free and kept going, weaving in and out of the crosses in his approach to the mission.

Someone was sure to speak up now, but who would it be? A young pupil? A village elder? A laborer from the fields? One of the kindly—

"What's this all about?"

The shout came from behind, and Mary spun, knowing by the voice who it was.

Jack Landon!

He approached on a ridden-down roan with white lather across its neck and shoulders, but the horse looked no less worn than he did. His cheeks were flushed and he had bags under his eyes, as if he hadn't slept well in days. And yet he seemed a powerful figure against the sky as he held his head up defiantly and gained the attention of the rangers.

"You back for silver dollars?" he accused.

"They will burn the mission!" Mary told him.

Jack Landon turned first to her, and then to the buck-toothed ranger who now stood looking back from outside the mission doors, but it was the sergeant named Wolfe who he addressed.

"You don't burn down a church!"

Wolfe hacked up phlegm and spat under his bay's breast. "*You,* huh? Some nerve you got, writing that pack of lies in the El Paso paper. Our man Riggs come down to have it out with you. Next thing we know, he's floating dead in the river. We're getting answers, one way or another!"

This time, Jack Landon didn't deny authorship. "If your problem's with me, then leave these people and their church alone!"

He brought his horse forward, and Mary ushered her students out of the way. As he passed, she noticed a spiny cholla twisted in the roan's tail, a dull green stalk amid red horse hairs, and she wondered where he had taken the animal. He continued on toward the rangers, the stalk swinging with the roan's gait as the crowd parted to let him through.

As Jack Landon neared Wolfe, the latter placed a precautionary hand on the grip of his holstered revolver.

"You the one killed him?" Wolfe challenged.

"Look at my face."

Mary could see only the back of Jack Landon's head now, but she knew what he meant. As the days had passed, his pistol-whipped features had looked increasingly frightful, thanks to the purple bruising around the still-healing cuts across his brow and beside his eye.

He drew rein before Wolfe. "Riggs was in Esperanza, all right, and he took his pound of flesh. You think I was in any condition to do anything about it?"

Wolfe drew his revolver and trained it on him. "Keep your damned hands where I can see them. You're going with us." He turned to the nearby rangers. "Cuff him!"

No!

In terrible fear, Mary could only watch helplessly as rangers searched Jack Landon's person and handcuffed him. But before they could lead him away, she called on a nearby woman to watch after the children and then pushed hurriedly through the assembly.

"He has done nothing!" she cried. "He is our teacher—he has done nothing!"

The rangers made no response, but Jack Landon looked around at her. "It's all right, Mary." He forced a smile that seemed incongruous with his bruising and lacerations. "Maybe he'll come back now."

And then he was gone, as suddenly as he had appeared outside the window of her home all those months ago.

As the rangers, riding in front and back, escorted Jack out of Esperanza and north into rugged country under the Candelaria Rim, he heard his heart and intellect tell him the same thing over the rattle of saddles and the rhythmic beat of hoofs.

He was out of Mary's life, and it was for the best.

For a while, she had given him a reason for being, but now he supposed it didn't matter what these lawless men who called themselves Texas Rangers did to him. This way, Roberto would be free to return, and Mary could cling to the boy who was more a son to her than a brother. She could mold him into the man their father had been, and Roberto in return would show her the respect and love that she deserved.

Or so hope whispered, even as circumstances had again cast Jack adrift on a dark, uncaring road whose end would be *his* end, whether today or tomorrow or forty purposeless years from now.

But as he rocked in the saddle and steadied himself against the horn with his secured hands, he still had enough of a reporter's mindset to know truth from a lie.

He loved Mary, and he hadn't had the courage to admit it to both of them and accept the consequences.

For the love of her, and for his adopted home of Esperanza, he had been through hell since he had met with the Intelligence Police captain at Candelaria on Wednesday. The officer clearly had suspected that Jack had known more about his informant's whereabouts than he had revealed. Indeed, Jack had ridden away stricken with fear that the Eighth Cavalry would follow him back and ravage Esperanza in a misguided operation to root out its supposed bandit element.

As a result, Jack had turned downstream instead and veered

away from the river into badlands. For two days and nights, he had circled back through a corner of perdition ruled by twisting arroyos and sandy expanses of gypsum and quartz that lay like strange snow under bare ridges with jagged rimrock. Twice, he had sighted the dust plumes of pursuers, but through cacti and across sterile wasteland he had pushed on, a man guilty for allowing only minimal rest for a horse that wasn't even his.

By a route that couldn't be traced, Jack had ultimately reached Esperanza—only to discover that rangers had swooped upon the village and shaken its people with a threat that not even the Eighth Cavalry would have made. Now these same unscrupulous men had him in custody, but at least he had done one last thing for the village and deflected suspicion from its blameless residents.

As midday approached at a point a hundred yards past a spring, Jack's captors drew rein at a great, rugged rock cradled in sotol hills and rent by an uneven V with mining tailings. Twenty yards to the right of the cleft, a roofless stone ruin projected from the rock to stand between upright boulders that, like the dark cliff at the rear, formed part of the high walls that seemed without windows. It was a desolate place, and the sun beat down with a silent rage, its heat radiating from the surrounding slopes as if unaware that tomorrow was the winter solstice.

Back in Esperanza, Jack had recognized Wolfe immediately by the odd way the scruffy ranger had kept his head cocked, like a dog trying to assess a situation. Now, as Jack and the riders dismounted, he scanned the faces and identified two other men who had taken part in the extortion ploy against Father Diego.

One had a deformed nose, as if broken once and never set, and as he squatted on his heels and lifted his horse's forefoot, he sucked on his stained buckteeth. The second ranger, a bull of a man with a thick neck, removed his hat, revealing a beetled brow dripping with sweat. After wiping it against his sleeve, he proceeded to flap his grimy hat against his leg, making the dust fly.

Jack was still taking in details when rough hands seized the front of his peon shirt and drove him back against the fender of his saddle, spooking the roan.

"How'd our man wind up dead?" demanded Wolfe.

Startled, his heart hammering against the man's fists, Jack could only stare. But the ranger was in no mood to be patient, and the five-and-one-half-inch barrel of his revolver swung up.

"Maybe this will help you remember," Wolfe snapped.

He twisted the Colt before Jack's face, intimidating but never pointing, the steel coming to life in the sunlight.

Jack glanced at the ruin and managed a breath. "I see you dragged me off out here where there's not any witnesses. Glad I mailed the letters I did on Wednesday."

"What the hell you—?"

"Candelaria. The Intelligence Police told me they found a ranger in the river. Been shot, but it wasn't even a mortal wound, they said, so who knows what happened. With the run-in I'd had with Riggs, I figured I might get blamed. The way you've been extorting people, I didn't think you'd be much for due process, so I wrote Austin again, the *El Paso Morning Times,* and said if I end up dead, they'd know who was responsible."

After a pause for dramatic effect, Jack added, "It's Wolfe with an *E,* isn't it?"

"You SOB," said the ranger, lowering his Colt.

The man with the unusual dental features looked up from alongside his stirrup. "He ain't got *our* names, at least," he told the ranger who continued to flap his hat.

"Maybe not," Jack responded, "but how many of you have got buckteeth and a nose bent sideways? Or a brow ridge like he's got? See the rolls of skin under the back of his head? The

way I described the two of you—your horses too—you might as
well be wearing names across your backs."

The ranger with buckteeth jumped to his feet and turned to
Wolfe in alarm. "Sergeant . . . !"

Wolfe released his grip on Jack's shirt, but not before shoving
him back against the roan a second time. "Think you're smarter
than us, don't you."

"How come Esperanza's such a target of yours?" asked Jack.
"You've been strong-arming the priest. They're just hardworking people trying to get by."

"Like hell. They're squatters and thieves. Ask any of the
ranchers. Ain't got no right to be there, grazing their goats on
somebody else's land. Every last one of them needs to go back
across the river where they come from."

"Most of the people were born in Esperanza. They're as
American as you and me."

"Damned bandits is what they are. All these raids—we can
trace it right back to that den of snakes, like Captain Fox says."

Jack thought of Román and Natividad, but nevertheless
pressed the issue. "You've got evidence?"

When Wolfe didn't come up with a response, Jack went on.

"You're grouping Esperanza with lawlessness out of Mexico
because they've got a common heritage. I made that point in
my letter Wednesday."

Wolfe spat between Jack's sandals. "Think anybody 'cept
Riggs paid any mind to you before? Bet the adjutant general's
still laughing about it."

"I didn't bother with the adjutant general this time. This letter went straight to the governor, with copies to his political op-
ponents in case he ignores it."

Out of nowhere flashed a hard fist, and the next thing Jack
knew, he was down beside shifting hoofs, the crushed rock searing his ear. Men were scuffling above him, and he lifted his

head to the bright sky and saw Wolfe trying to pull the beetle-browed ranger away.

"Needs finishin' off!" yelled the restrained man, missing with a vicious kick. "Let me at him!"

"Settle down!" ordered Wolfe.

But Jack's assailant was determined, and he grazed Jack's thigh with a powerful boot.

"Quit it!" joined in the ranger with buckteeth. "Somethin' happens to him, they's comin' after us!"

The burly man continued to fume, but eventually he stalked away wagging his bulbous head and cursing. Meanwhile, Wolfe's silhouette weaved back and forth across the blinding sun as he hovered over Jack and pressured him again for answers about Riggs.

"There's nothing to tell," Jack persisted.

Except that justice was done! The bastard intended to outrage Mary!

Wolfe glanced over his shoulder at the hulking ranger, who continued to swear as he paced alongside the ruin.

"If you was a greaser, I'd let him beat it out of you," Wolfe told Jack. Then he checked the fiery wheel that blazed in the sky. "Let's see how stubborn you are after a couple of days in this sun without no water. Get up!"

CHAPTER 19

Mary was alone in the world.

First, she had lost her mother and father, two tragedies separated by fifteen years. Then in rapid succession, Roberto had fled Esperanza, and Jack Landon had been taken away to an unknown fate. Now she had no one, and inside her was a void that swelled with every passing moment.

And the person whose loss contributed most to it was someone about whom she had never taken measure of her feelings.

No matter whether he had a place for her in his life, she had a place in hers for Jack Landon.

Mary had never realized it until she stood watching the rangers drag him away, the dust of their horses shrouding her last glimpse of him. The revelation drove her to dismiss the students for the Christmas break and follow on the dapple gray that was still healing from its forefoot injury. She had no delusions that anything she could do would make a difference—not in the face of seven armed men—but she would regret it the rest of her life if she did nothing.

As she rode, the self-defeating thoughts began to recede, replaced by an assurance that she would never be truly alone—not when Jesucristo went with her.

He was at her side as she traced the upside-down *U's* of eight sets of hoofs through winding drainages and up across ridges where the azure Candelaria Rim provided a dramatic backdrop to bear grass and century plants. He went with her through le-chuguilla and ocotillo, and past sotol and twisted Spanish daggers. She seemed to need His presence most as the dapple gray brushed stirrup-high *sangre de drago* or dragon's blood, and navigated stretches of devil's claw, devil's head, and devil cholla. Like the horned lizards creeping among the rocks, they served as reminders that hers was a fight not just against flesh and blood.

Two hours into the backcountry, Mary noticed a subtle dip in the horse's nose with the dapple gray's four-beat gait across a hogback. For a few paces she disregarded it, not wanting to admit the truth. When she dismounted, she found the animal standing with a front hoof forward and tipped on edge, a stance her father had called "pointing."

The animal had aggravated its injury, and Mary closed her welling eyes to the picturesque wall of the Candelaria Rim and accepted that when God wills, even the saints are powerless.

Night had fallen by the time she approached Esperanza with the lame house in tow. Over the village hung a quarter moon, the adobes barely outlined in its pale light. Spent as she passed under the point of sentinel hill, she was surprised to find the mission windows aglow on her left. Inside, silhouettes moved against the candles burning in the sconces, and as she came abreast of the courtyard's west wall, she saw figures coming and going through the mission doors.

Perplexed, Mary went around to the arched gate, where she tied the dapple gray before starting through the graveyard. Outside the mission doors, she met seventy-two-year-old Longino Castaneda, the white-bearded village patriarch whom everyone affectionately called *Tío,* or Uncle.

"*¡Mi Mariposita!*" he exclaimed. "San Miguel has watched over you!"

For as long as Mary could remember, she had been Mariposita, Little Butterfly, to Tío Longino. He indeed served the role of an uncle to everyone, for he was a kind and caring man with an infectious smile that showed missing teeth. He had been her father's closest friend, and on the night that Mary had lost her mother, Tío had rushed to their home and mourned with them.

Then eight months ago, when news of her father's death had broken, an inconsolable Tío had fought through a violent windstorm to reach her door, and she would never forget his quivering lips and the rivulets on his deeply scored cheeks. Now he wrapped her in his gnarly arms and thanked the archangel Saint Michael for her safe return.

"What is happening here, Tío?" she asked, peering over his hunched shoulder at the closed double doors.

"We pray for Señor Landon." Turning, he swung back a door for her. "Come and see, Mariposita."

She entered, and surely enough, they were there, kneeling between the benches, their hands clenched in prayerful poses under bowed heads, the collective whispers of their appeals like the rushing wind of *Espirtu Santo* on the first Pentecost. She saw Father Diego, priest and steward, on whose behalf Jack Landon had stood up to lawless men who had long bled Esperanza of its silver. She saw Señora Ramos, the still-grieving mother without a child, whom Jack Landon had befriended and then defended against a soulless ranger. She saw Jack Landon's students, six eager-to-learn girls beside grateful parents who recognized the chance he had given them to rise above squalor.

One and all, these parishioners no longer would live under the shadow of flood, and they constituted a cross section of an entire village impacted in some way by a person from another culture who, at the end, had shouldered blame that wasn't his to protect this very sanctuary.

Mary was touched beyond words, and the empty place in her

heart where Jack Landon had lived was now greater than she could bear. Her head hanging, she edged between right-side benches and sank to her knees in prayer that Our Lady and all the saints would guard him.

"Our Little Mary has come back."

From the aisle, Tío Longino's voice quieted the petitions.

"Mariposita," he continued, "what can you tell us?"

Mary turned, finding the patriarch at her shoulder and all the faces across the aisle looking at her. Brushing her cheeks, she rose before a people who had so little, and yet were wealthy in the things that really mattered.

"It is in the hands of Jesucristo," she said through the emotion. "My horse could go no farther."

She wanted to say more. She wanted to thank each of them by name, and ask Father Diego to bless them for their ministrations. But the words would not come, and she welcomed Tío Longino's arms about her and listened as Esperanza prayed for Jack Landon.

From outside the rock ruin that held him prisoner, the sound of arguing stirred Jack from restless sleep.

It was Monday, December 24, and above him where a roof should have been—past sheer, twelve-foot walls—the sun flared in the midday sky. Its direct rays were ruthless in this window-less box that had once been quarters for miners, and even as Jack sat scrunched in the thin shade beside the weathered door, the radiating heat was almost unbearable.

Three days before, in front of Wolfe and six other reprobate rangers, Jack had acted out the bluff of his life. After meeting with the Intelligence Police in Candelaria, he had written no one—not the *El Paso Morning Times,* not the governor, not the governor's political enemies.

And he still didn't know if his ruse would be enough.

As he had approached Esperanza after the torturous journey from Candelaria, Jack had slaked his thirst at a spring. Even so, the ensuing ride in handcuffs to this place had parched him again, and upon his incarceration he had endured brutal day after brutal day without water.

Suffering, Jack knew he couldn't last much longer. He hadn't urinated for more hours than he could remember. His throat burned as if he had swallowed a coal hot off a fire. His heart raced and he breathed with quick, shallow breaths. When he pinched the back of his hand, the skin had lost its elasticity. Now, as he edged light-headed toward the door and the voices beyond, the walls seemed to float away from their moorings.

Strangely, he wondered if this was the way Jesus of Nazareth had felt when he had spoken of his thirst from a Roman cross outside Jerusalem nineteen hundred years ago.

Even as Jack pressed his face to the door's splintery wood and peered through a crack, he heard the argument persist between the man with buckteeth and a second ranger who also had been left to guard. Repeatedly over the days, they had pressed Jack for answers about Riggs's death, and each time, he had resolutely denied knowledge. Now they shouted at one another, something about Wolfe and the fact that it was Monday noon and the concern that Jack could succumb if things didn't change.

"No skin off *your* damned nose if he dies!" said the ranger with buckteeth. "He ain't wrote nobody what *you* look like. Help me get this rock rolled away from the door. We's gettin' out of here. Captain Fox won't hold it against us."

Jack withdrew in fear that his interest might alter the dynamics for the worse. Soon he heard rock grating against rock, accompanied by grunts and profanity just as discordant. Finally hoofs began to drum, and when they receded out of earshot, he pushed open the creaking door to find the small, black boulder between him and a smoldering campfire. Pulling himself up with a hand on the jamb, he stumbled out like a cowboy on a big drunk at the saloon next to the *San Angelo Daily Standard.*

The odor of broiled venison had wafted through the ruin all morning, and an entire brisket still sizzled alongside open tin cans on the upright rocks of the fire ring. But Jack needed water, and he needed it desperately, and he staggered down the beaten trace for the spring he had noticed three days before.

Jack would never have believed that a mere hundred yards could be so demanding. The ground wouldn't stay in place, instead seeming to ebb and flow, and he weaved across it with head down, the only way to keep the world from going dark. To fall might mean he would never rise again, so he persevered a step at a time, just as he had wrenched a word at a time out of his typewriter for so many years.

The trickling of water guided him the last few feet across a dark slab of rough rock to a break between low, jumbled boulders. The sky showed in a small pool before him, and as he sprawled on his stomach, the change in angle presented the reflection of cattails and maidenhair ferns growing in the shallows beyond.

Only now did he realize that his unsaddled roan was staked nearby, within reach of both water and forage in the form of tobosa grass and black grama. But Jack was focused on survival. Burying his face in the pool, he drank, and he continued to gulp to excess until his stomach cramped. He had no choice but to roll over and shield his eyes from the glare, but as soon as the pain subsided, he quenched his thirst again, this time more prudently.

For hours, it seemed, Jack drank and cramped and rested, but ultimately he improved enough to return to the fire. He had gone so long without eating that he had no appetite, but now the aroma of food restored his hunger. Soon he was partaking of not only venison, but leftover tortillas and unfinished cans of beans and corned beef. With every nourishing bite, a measure of his vigor came back, but he had been through an ordeal from which he would need time to recover.

With day fading, and the way back to Esperanza unmarked, Jack did the sensible thing. Building up the fire against the approaching chill of Christmas Eve night, he stretched out beside the circle of charred rocks and stared at the blaze. Strangely, he seemed to see Román in those lapping flames, and hear in the popping wood the words the miscreant had let slip. Concerned, Jack fell into a deep sleep plagued by distressing dreams of what the coming day might mean for the misguided brother of a girl he loved.

CHAPTER 20

The way was gloomy on this predawn morning of December 25, 1917, but Roberto's father seemed a guiding light who beckoned him to pull his horse out of this march of forty Banderos Colorados riders bent for Brite Ranch.

In one short week, Roberto had come to see them for what they were. They were a loathsome bunch, without loyalty to Carranza or Villa or anything but their own lusts. To hear them tell it, they were the victims of injustice who deserved whatever they could wrench from men who had more—especially gringos. Not a one was willing to accept any responsibility for his lot in life, and they seemed incapable of appreciating the finer qualities in a man like Roberto's father. Roberto could only imagine the disrespect his sister would provoke.

But he was here, choking in the dust raised by their horses, a muchacho questioning the choices that had led him to this stretch of road up and over the Candelaria Rim. At first light, they would raid Brite headquarters, an isolated American settlement in a high desert grassland under the sawtooth ridge of Capote Mountain. This three-mile-wide valley, just under a mile in elevation, would echo with gunshots, and blood would spill.

But would Roberto's role in it be a matter of avenging his father, or dishonoring him?

Abruptly, the riders ahead slowed and began to bunch. Roberto halted with them, and as the trailing alkali caught up and hung in his throat with a taste more bitter than ever, he found himself alongside Román and Natividad. Between silhouetted riders, Roberto saw the muted light of a three-quarter moon on the breast of a rider who had wheeled his horse and now faced everyone. Roberto knew this lieutenant of Chico Cano's as Gold Buttons, for he wore an old Carrancista uniform with shiny ornaments down the front.

To the left of Gold Buttons, Roberto could see a dark embankment, perhaps a dam for an earthen tank, while a quarter mile beyond the bandit, shadows and contrasting moonlight traced out the small settlement at Brite. Roberto had been told that here was not only ranch headquarters with its outlying structures, but also a post office and store. Indeed, his father had come to Brite Store shortly before his death, and he had returned to Esperanza and told of the merchant's stock of shoes called Hamilton-Brown made in some far-off place.

As Roberto waited nervously, his palms sweating despite the chill, Gold Buttons outlined the plan of attack and divided the bandits accordingly. Roberto, he ordered to stay back and guard this road up from the distant river with Román, Natividad, and a scar-faced man in his thirties named Gonzales. Román quietly grumbled his displeasure, but Roberto suspected it was mere bluster; Román had never faced gunfire the way he had on that day in Mexico with Jack Landon.

Jack Landon.

Strangely, Roberto's teacher was very much on his mind. In class, Mister Landon had laid out the character of the bandits exactly as Roberto had found them, but the muchacho had been too stubborn to listen. More importantly, Mister Landon had helped him discover his role model, and had encouraged him to test every choice with a simple question: *What would your papá do in your place?*

Now, as the other raiders rode on and left the four of them to wait in the javelina bushes and sotol stalks to the right of the road, Roberto asked himself that very thing.

Gonzales was a detestable man with whom Roberto's father never would have allied. The bandit was bad-tempered and vulgar, an unkempt, reeking animal whose demeanor made Roberto ashamed to stand shoulder to shoulder with him in the dawning light of a day that would gauge his own worth as the son of his papá.

This was where Roberto had ended up.

This was what his upbringing by the best of men had bred.

This was the first day of the rest of his life.

Just before sunrise, gunfire at headquarters broke the stillness. The first shot came from a rifle, and it precipitated such a barrage that Roberto could barely tell one report from another. Soon, however, he could distinguish carbines and six-shooters and a shotgun, a grim chorus of which his father would have had no part.

And through it all, as terrified voices cried out and gun smoke drifted across the settlement, Gonzales stood laughing—laughing at an attack on innocent people on the day Jesucristo had been born.

Eventually, the battle died down until there were only occasional rifle shots, and then none at all. As Roberto watched in bright sunlight from his guard post, figures gathered at what appeared to be two attached adobe buildings with high, A-shaped roofs. Soon an ax began to impact the door, the echoes no less distinct than the gunshots had been.

"The store, Román?" asked Natividad.

Looking on, his brother breathed sharply. "The *pendejos* will get everything," he complained. "They leave me here to bark like a dog."

Suddenly, to a pop louder than the distant ax, Román was down at Gonzales's feet. Turning, Roberto realized that the bandit's open hand against Román's skull had put him there.

Considering all the times the teenager had demeaned Roberto, he didn't feel sorry for him, even as Román wallowed and moaned and clutched his ear.

Gonzales kicked Román and bellowed a vicious epithet. "You don't like things? Tell Cano and see what happens, eh?"

A rumble rose up from back along the road, and Roberto discovered dust billowing from an approaching wagon. Pulled by two horses, the hack had spindly corner poles that supported a top, and canvas siding that was rolled up to allow air to flow freely. Inside were three occupants, jostled by the wheels that churned to the clomp of hoofs.

"*Cabrón!*" exclaimed Gonzales. He motioned Roberto and Natividad to their mounts. "Stop the *bastardos!*"

The Bisley Model Colt inside Roberto's rope belt gouged his abdomen as he swung across his roan. He no longer wanted anything to do with this, but a quick look at Román dazed on the ground told him he was out of options.

Papa! What do I do, Papa? Papa!

At the edge of the road, he held his horse alongside Natividad's and watched the hack grow nearer. The driver was a gringo, dressed in a shirt as white as Roberto's, and behind him sat two men of Mexican heritage. With the gunfire over, the three displayed no concern even as Natividad crossed the road and waited on the other side. But as the team came abreast of Roberto with a jangling of trace chains, and he and the other muchacho fell in alongside the leggy horses, the driver must have wondered.

Then Natividad seized the far animal by the throat latch, and Roberto had no choice but to do the same with the nearer horse, and there was no longer any pretense.

"What's the meaning of this?" shouted the driver.

But even as a whip cracked across horse flesh, Roberto held fast to the throat latch until the hack was dead in the dust-clouded road.

"I'm carrying the U.S. mail!" continued the driver. "What the hell you—"

A revolver thundered, spooking Roberto's roan. He spun as the team tried to bolt, the throat latch digging into his hand, and he saw Gonzales running up alongside the hack and gun smoke trailing from his six-shooter.

"*Abajo!* Down!" yelled Gonzales, lacing his order with profanity in two languages.

Now the occupants reacted not only with alarm, but fear, and it was especially true of the two Mexican passengers behind the driver.

"*¡No me hagas daño!*" pleaded the nearer man, fumbling with the low side door. "*Por favor,* Gonzales! Don't hurt me!"

The bandit brandished his six-shooter. "Who else is in there?" He cocked his head to see around him. "Both of you *cabróns* know me, eh?"

Suddenly the second passenger was scrambling away, and just as suddenly another shot startled the team and the man fell limp across the opposite side board.

Stunned, Roberto could only cling to the throat latch and watch, but for a moment all he could see was his father, cradled in the arms of Jesucristo beyond a sky that had gone as dark as the day of the crucifixion. Roberto was an accomplice to a heinous act—an unwilling accomplice, but if his father was looking down on him now, it was with shame.

"*Por favor! Por favor!*" begged the nearer passenger.

With a cry, Roberto reined his roan about and charged the animal for Gonzales. In two strides the horse was there, bowling the bandit over, but simultaneously the revolver discharged and the nearer passenger fell against the side door. The force pushed it open, draping the man facedown across the edge of the wagon bed, his hanging arms almost touching the ground.

Roberto wheeled his horse and checked Gonzales sprawled under the roan's neck, only to see the bandit's revolver flash up and the muzzle explode fire. A powerful, unseen force twisted Roberto in the saddle, a blow so numbing that he felt nothing at all at first.

But as he fell across the roan's neck, he instinctively gigged the horse into flight, and the animal's legs reached out again and again for the far-off river as bullets whizzed and peppered the road.

CHAPTER 21

On into late afternoon on Tuesday, Christmas Day, Mary maintained the prayer vigil before the mission altar.

Since Friday, other villagers had come and gone, but she had spent every waking hour here, petitioning Jesucristo and the saints to bring back Jack Landon and watch over her brother. Mary did not fault the other parishioners for their absence; they had lives of their own and families with needs to address. Only Tío Longino, a widower, had sat with her throughout the four days, and the comfort of his presence was immeasurable.

After midnight Mass on Christmas Eve, Mary had decided against returning home to sleep, choosing instead to devote the coming holy day to even greater prayer. Still, Tío had stayed with her, sleeping at her elbow as his peaceful, old-man snoring had fluttered the long white whiskers around his open mouth. Now he sat up and turned to her.

"Go home and rest, Mariposita," he urged in his quavering voice. "Our Lady will carry your prayers to Jesucristo."

"I must stay and pray."

The *viejo* smiled a toothless smile. "You love Jack Landon *mucho*, no?"

Taken by surprise, Mary could only look at him.

"You think I didn't know?" he added.

Mary didn't know how to respond. All she knew was that she felt sadder than ever as she continued to listen.

"You're my little butterfly that I watch over for your papá."

Now, a passing sadness came over the old man too, and he began to blink more than necessary. "I see the smile when you're with the young señor. But for a week before the rangers came, you were always alone and your smile was gone. A quarrel between two young people in love, Mariposita?"

"Between two, Tío?"

"*Sí.* He loves you just as much."

Mary held her stare. "Why do you—?"

The *viejo* placed a gnarled hand on her shoulder. "An hombre doesn't live this long without learning things. The young señor looks at you the way your papá looked at your mother." He crossed himself. "Bless their souls."

Mary began to weep.

"Go home and rest, little one," Tío urged. "It is what the young señor would want."

Nevertheless, Mary would have stayed, even though she had fought the weight of her eyelids for hours. But the old man was insistent.

"Go home and rest. Go home and rest."

"Only if we both go home, Tío."

The *viejo* just smiled, but when she started for the mission doors, he followed in his shambling gait.

As Mary pushed open a door and faced the glare, movement off to the left seized her attention. A roan horse was disappearing around an adobe that blocked the school, and although she merely glimpsed the rider, what she saw took away her breath.

"*¡Mira!*" exclaimed Tío Longino from over her shoulder. "Does that not look like—?"

"It *is*, Tío. It *is*!"

With newfound energy, Mary rushed through the graveyard and under the arched gate, her pulse racing to a name she whispered over and over. She hurried past the adobe and reached the school, and when she burst around the attached residence, he was there, hitching the roan to a post just past the door.

"Jack Landon! Jack Landon!"

He looked up as she ran through the chickens, the down flying as the squawking hens flapped their wings and scattered. He was thin and drawn and burned by the sun, and he called her name hoarsely as if his throat was as cooked as his cracked lips.

"Jesucristo has brought you back!" she cried as she opened her arms.

"You may not want to touch me till I clean up," he warned.

Mary did not care. He was smiling, and she fell into his arms and laid her head on his shoulder. If she could have embraced him forever, she would have done so.

"God has been good to me! You were dead, Jack Landon!"

"Almost. They kept me without water. They let me loose yesterday, but I was too weak to come back till today."

He pulled away far enough so they could look at one another. Hers was a flurry of emotions, and she supposed that she expressed them in the only way she could, for he brushed her cheek with his thumb.

"I saw the mission's still here," he said. "For a while I was afraid they'd ride back and burn it out of meanness."

"You do not know what Esperanza has done for you. You do not know that the village has taken our prayers to the altar every day and night, and that the Mother of God has delivered them to Jesucristo. He has listened, and He has answered."

"Day and night? You mean a vigil?"

"Tío Longino stayed with me when no one else was able."

Jack Landon was evidently struck by all that she had said. Withdrawing, he looked away and seemed to stare past the far edge of his adobe. Maybe he focused on things unseen, but against the sky under the eave, Mary could see the cross atop the nearby bluff.

"Since Friday?" he asked quietly. "The entire village?"

"You have done much for Esperanza, Jack Landon."

He faced her. "It's done more for me. You especially. Like the first time we were up at the cross together and I told you how my mother died. Ever since then, I've started to see things differently. I don't even think about that night anymore."

"Praise be to God for your peace!"

"I guess I've reconciled with myself about what happened to her."

"You did what you had to for her. There was nothing else you could have done!"

"I see that now. Just being around you's changed things for me that way, and when those rangers were dragging me away like they did, I wished I'd told you what you mean to me."

She wanted to press near him again, but she hesitated.

"What *do* I mean to you, Jack Landon?"

He stretched out his hand and took hers, and now she wasn't the only one overcome by emotion.

"I know what I said about leaving," he rasped. "I know how much getting your brother back would mean to you. But when things were at their worst and I knew they were about to kill me, I just wanted one more chance to tell you that . . ."

For only a moment, he hesitated.

"I'm not waiting any longer to say it, Mary. I love you."

"Mariposita! Señor Landon!"

Mary had no chance to process the moment. She spun at Tío Longino's cry of alarm and saw him round the corner of the adobe simultaneous with the nose of a horse. She wanted to ask what was wrong, but before she could form the words, another pace of the lathered roan brought a slumping rider into view.

"Roberto! Mother of God!"

Mary didn't even remember running, but she found herself abreast of the horse and reaching for him. His white cotton garments, ragged in the breast, glistened with fresh blood, and when he turned his head she saw why. It oozed from frightful wounds in his left cheek and under his chin, as well as from an exposed laceration where his right nipple should have been.

Panicked, Mary could only say his name over and over, and then Jack Landon was at her shoulder, supporting her brother as Tío led the horse to the door. There, while the *viejo* hitched the animal, the two of them helped Roberto dismount as his soaked garments smeared the fender of the saddle.

Roberto was attempting to say something, whether in Spanish or English she couldn't tell, for between his lips she could see a loose segment of bloody gum with teeth in it.

"I cannot understand you, my brother! I cannot understand!"

"I think a bullet grazed his chest and went under his chin and out his jaw," Jack Landon told her. "Took out part of the bone and it's in the way of him trying to talk. What is it you're saying, Roberto?"

Still, the words were unintelligible, but when he simulated the act of drinking, Mary understood.

"*Agua!* He wants water!"

Jack Landon nodded to the door. "On through to the kitchen there's a jug. Bring the shears, too, while Tío and I get him in the house."

Mary did as he directed, and when she scurried back, they had sat Roberto down on the clay floor just inside the threshold and Jack Landon was bent over him, examining his mouth.

"I have water, my brother!"

"The shears first," Jack Landon appealed.

Mary passed a clean linen bundle and dropped to her knees to help however she might. Jack Landon reassured her as he unwrapped the shears.

"Boiled them last week after cutting up a chicken." He turned his attention to her brother. "This is going to hurt some, Roberto. That hanging piece of gum's got to come out or you'll choke."

Jack Landon's hand was already covered with blood, but he used his fingers to pry open her brother's mouth and worked the shears inside. Roberto began to strangle and slap at Jack Landon's arms, and all Mary could do was beg her brother to stop while she helped Tío restrain him.

It was an awful half-minute that seemed to last forever, but finally Jack Landon withdrew a bloody section of bone and gum with three teeth imbedded. When he tossed it out the door, a dozen chickens broke for it and contended over the prize until a hen grabbed it and ran away.

Mary placed a cup of water in Roberto's hands and guided it to his lips. "Sips, my brother. A little at a time."

"Now maybe you feel better, little muchacho?" asked Tío.

But after a few gurgling swallows, Roberto declined any more and Mary helped lay him back. For a few seconds, she let her hand linger against his hot forehead.

"We need to clean the wounds, Mary," said Jack Landon. "Would you be able to sew him up?" Then he addressed the old man. "Tío Longino, he's in a lot of pain. Can you find something to dull it?"

"Ah, *tequila*. I will be back *a toda prisa*, quickly."

For a moment, Mary stroked her brother's hair. "I will go brew *toloache*, nightshade, for your fever, Roberto. And grind masa out of sagebrush for your wounds."

A step ahead of Tío, Mary hastened out the door, so many things competing for her thoughts.

CHAPTER 22

For an hour now, the two of them had tended Roberto on the clay floor.

Jack had supported the boy's shoulders while Mary had poured *tequila* down his throat for the pain, and *toloache* for the fever. With fresh water from the plaza well, they had cleaned his chest and cheek and the underside of his chin. Jack had stabilized the muchacho's head so that she could close the wounds with needle and thread, and after the stitching was completed and she had sprinkled ground sagebrush, they had brushed fingers in applying bandages. As the chickens outside the door retreated to their roosts and Tío Longino held a kerosene lamp close, they continued to work shoulder to shoulder to address the suffering boy's needs.

But no matter how often Jack glanced at her, Mary still wouldn't make eye contact.

Maybe Jack had violated a rule of conduct. Maybe there were things better left unsaid in a friendship. Maybe an open avowal of his feelings had added too many complexities, and they could never go back to the way things had been.

Jack didn't know, and it bothered him even as Roberto clutched Mary's arm and did his best to talk. The muchacho's tongue was numbed by pain and thickened by *tequila,* and at first neither of them could understand, but as the boy persisted, Jack pieced together muddy words in Spanish.

"I tried to stop him, Marita. For Papa, I would have stopped all of them!"

"Stopped who, my brother? Who did this to you?"

"They are bad men—very bad men."

"Wait—isn't this Christmas Day?" interjected Jack. "Have you been with Román, Roberto? His brother? Have you been with Los Banderos Colorados somewhere you shouldn't?"

For the first time since Roberto had shown up covered in blood, Mary turned in Jack's direction.

"Why do you ask, Jack Landon?"

But Jack was busy pressing her brother. "Where was it? One of the mines? A wax factory?"

Now the boy struggled more than ever to form words. "I tried to stop him. I did what Papa would have done!"

The muchacho became increasingly agitated and began to thrash, and Jack knew that if it continued, he might tear open his fragile stitches. Still, with what Jack had been through to protect Roberto, he felt he had a right to answers—even at the expense of a badly wounded boy.

"I want the truth," he pushed. "I almost died protecting you, and you're going to tell me!"

The effects of Jack's six-day ordeal that had begun at Candelaria had bred impatience, and impatience was giving way to hostility. Jack knew it, and he realized that Mary knew it, even before she spoke.

"Please do not upset him that way!"

"He's been riding with bandits!" Jack replied without turning. Abruptly he found himself shaking the muchacho. "You shoot somebody first, Roberto? That what happened?"

"You are hurting him!" exclaimed Mary.

But Jack was too caught up in the moment, and his hands became rougher on the boy's shoulders. "You answer me, Roberto!"

"Stop!" cried Mary.

Then delicate fingers seized Jack's arm and he regained control. As he removed his hands from the boy and turned, he and Mary finally made eye contact, and Jack didn't like what he saw.

"Let my brother rest!" she said.

She had never upbraided him before, and whether he deserved it or not, he was too spent to be tolerant. Without another word, he rose to storm away, only to find that he had no place to go in his own home except out into the dusk.

Once there, Jack exhausted the last of his energy and returned the horses to their respective pens in the village. For a long while afterward, he sat in the dark against the rock cone of the plaza well and considered what he had done, and when he started back, angry at himself and penitent, he met a creaking wagon with a hunched figure in the seat.

"Tío Longino, that you?" he asked.

"*Sí.*"

The *viejo* said more as the wagon continued its slow rumble. But Jack didn't hear, for now he saw a boy lying in the wagon bed and a dainty form sitting on the tailgate.

"You didn't have to do that, Mary," said Jack. "You could have kept him where he was."

"Thanks be to God, you are safe," she said quietly. "But I will not let my brother stay with someone who hurts him."

Her blunt words lingered in the shadows as the wagon rolled past.

As great a mental toll as Jack had suffered, the days of torture had exacted a greater physical price.

He didn't know how late it was before he went to sleep on Christmas night, but he never saw the sun the following day. When he did force himself to arise, he stayed up only long enough to light a lamp and eat, and then he collapsed in bed again. Sick from his ordeal, he was too weak to do anything else—except dwell on the flashing anger in Mary's eyes as she had justly berated him.

On through the morning of the twenty-seventh, Jack never left his home, but when he eventually ran out of water, he had no choice but to go to the plaza well with a bucket. He just hoped he would have the strength to carry it back.

As he approached the rock cone, he found Román and Natividad drawing up water via the squeaking pulley attached to the weathered overhead crossbeam. In the afternoon sunlight, there was something distinctive about the brothers as they leaned over the rim. When Jack spoke, even his voice was weak.

"Those store-bought shoes, Román?"

Indeed, beside the empty pail on the ground, their footwear was incongruous with the clothing of peons. Obviously manufactured, the leather shoes were clean and almost flawless.

Natividad was the first to look in Jack's direction. "Román," he whispered nervously, alerting the older teenager.

Román continued to pull the well rope. "I hear him."

"Hamilton-Brown, aren't they?" added Jack. The hardware store next to the *Daily Standard* had carried the brand, but San Angelo was almost three hundred miles away.

The pulley continued to screech.

"Don't see many Hamilton-Browns in this country," said Jack. "Where did you get them?"

The pockmarked older brother swore under his breath. "Go away, gringo."

"Need water."

Jack didn't have the stamina for a confrontation, but he nevertheless went up and stopped at Román's shoulder, an act meant to intimidate. It worked on the younger brother, for Natividad grew more apprehensive and scooted away. From close up, Jack checked the shoes below their dingy white trousers;

even a thin layer of dust couldn't dull the sheen.

"Never saw Hamilton-Browns at the Candelaria store," said Jack. "Where did you get them?"

Now the well bucket was within reach, suspended under the crossbeam and dripping, and Natividad drew it in and set about filling the pail. Clearly on edge, he spilled a portion and splattered his shoes with mud.

"Getting your shoes dirty, Natividad," remarked Jack. "Let's see, only other store this side of the Southern Pacific is at Brite Ranch, I'm told."

Natividad flashed Jack a wide-eyed look and spilled even more water, generating a stern reprimand from the older muchacho.

"¡Pendejo!" Again, Román lowered the well bucket over the rim. "Now we need more."

From far below came a quiet ripple of water, and as the pulley complained once more to Román's tug, Natividad's gaze kept shifting between Jack and his brother. Jack focused on the more unnerved of the two.

"Hear about Roberto riding in all bloody on Christmas, Natividad?"

Natividad jerked his head back.

" 'Wait till Christmas Day,' " continued Jack. "Isn't that what your brother said?"

Natividad clutched Román's arm.

Jack went on. " 'Not satisfied with gringo scraps'—remember him telling me that? 'Maybe Roberto will ride with us,' he said."

There was fright in Natividad's whisper. "Román . . . !"

"Where you three been, Natividad, coming back with shoes like that?" pushed Jack.

Natividad continued to mutter to his brother. "Why did you—?"

"Shut up!" admonished Román.

"Guess you'd had too much *tequila* to remember, Natividad," said Jack. "Your brother told me all about it. So how did Roberto get shot?"

Román spun. "It takes a man to get back what's ours! Not a muchacho who fights against us!"

He released the pulley rope with its burden, and from deep in the well came a splash as the full bucket struck water. Taking up the half-full pail, he shoved his brother toward the plaza's far side.

"*¡Vamos!*" Román ordered, starting away.

"Running off again, Román?" taunted Jack. "Why don't you make something of yourself instead of blaming somebody else for what you don't have?"

After watching them hurry away, the dust swirling about their suspicious shoes, Jack lifted his gaze toward Mary's concealed home and knew exactly whom to blame for what *he* might no longer have.

CHAPTER 23

The sun set and rose and set again, and Jack opened his eyes in the dusk of December 28 not even wanting to get out of bed. Regret and loneliness had darkened his dreams, and now they darkened his waking moments as well.

Since Christmas, he had struggled merely to stir about his home and tend his chickens, but now a black veil seemed to descend—or did it rise up out of deepest hell? Regardless, it was there, settling across him and choking the fragile hope that he had forged in this place.

Esperanza had been the end of nowhere, the -30- at the bottom of Jack's final news story, one that he had lived rather than written. But the village had also been a beginning, and no factor had been more responsible than Mary. Had he been well the last two days, he would have looked in on Roberto and tried to close the rift with her. As it was, he could feel the gulf grow wider by the moment, for her silence was deafening.

No matter Jack's cruel grip on her brother's shoulders, wasn't their friendship strong enough to overcome his offense? She had seen for herself Jack's physical distress, and yet hour after hour had passed without her calling through the door to check on his welfare. Even if she didn't value their relationship to the degree that he did, she had lauded his service to Esperanza. Could one intemperate moment erase all of that?

Jack lighted the lamp next to his bed and opened her father's Bible. A good man had found comfort in these tear-stained pages, even though he had been unable to read. Was the power of faith so strong that a man impaled on a Roman cross could reach across nineteen hundred years and touch a person that way?

To the smell of kerosene and the purr of a burning wick, to the rustle of pages and the howl of an outside wind, Jack studied and tried to understand, as he had for weeks. It wasn't that the Bible had failed the test of intellect; on the contrary, the messianic prophecies in the Old Testament seemed amazingly fulfilled in Jesus of Nazareth, despite being set down by two dozen men over a span of fifteen hundred years. What Jack couldn't grasp was the concept of a Creator permitting the rise of sin against Him, and then making provisions for reconciliation through the substitutionary death of His Son on the cross.

But maybe, pondered Jack, a created being couldn't be expected to comprehend the ways of his Creator, any more than a character in a novel could fathom the mind of the novelist. What was it the book of Isaiah quoted the Creator as saying?

When he thumbed through, the passage in Spanish jumped off the page, and there was only one way to translate it:

For as the heavens are higher than the earth, so are my ways higher than your ways, and my thoughts than your thoughts.

With intellect not a stumbling block, maybe comfort and peace—and especially acceptance of the will of a Higher Power in all matters—hinged on acknowledging that there were things beyond understanding, and then simply *choosing* to believe.

Jack wasn't there yet, but he felt better about life as he laid the Bible aside and rose. A nourishing meal buoyed his spirits more, and he resolved not to let another hour pass mired in regret. When he took up a stack of papers and went out into the night, a remorseful man on a mission, he felt stronger than he had in days. Indeed, with the recuperative powers of youth, he felt almost as robust as ever.

A norther had struck, blowing down from sentinel hill and whistling around the eaves of his home. Drawing his woolen *serape* around his shoulders, he set out across the village. It was only minutes to Mary's, but the walk and brisk air cleared the thoughts that had been muddled by days of sickness and inactivity. What he had known before in only a passing way was now a matter of grave importance, for a dark cloud hung over the adobes.

These were the homes of a caring and hardworking people who wanted merely to live their lives and avoid the war that pressed in on all sides, and yet the actions of a misguided muchacho and two cohorts might have placed everyone in jeopardy.

The streets seemed empty except for slinking dogs, but Jack checked for telltale signs—larger shadows that moved, or flashes of the full moon in bandoleers filled with cartridges. Pausing, he listened for hoofbeats or the rattle of saddles. The *yip-yip* of coyotes was nothing out of the ordinary, but just as he reached Mary's home and found lamplight showing through cracks in the shutters, the far-off scream of a panther startled him. Unnerved, his concern for the village outweighing personal matters, he pounded on the door with an urgency that was evident in his voice.

"Mary! Mary!"

There was no immediate response, and he continued to call until the door swung inward and she appeared, a faceless figure against the lamplight.

"There's things I need to say to you," he said, "but first we've got to talk about Esperanza."

"Thank God you are all right!"

"Esperanza," Jack repeated.

"What about Esperanza?"

Jack glanced over his shoulder. "If there's been a raid, the village is the first place the Rangers will look to blame. I think the store at Brite Ranch was hit. I saw Román and Natividad with new Hamilton-Brown shoes on, and I think they got them from there."

"Roberto did not come back with such shoes," she contended.

"I think he was there and tried to stop it and the bandits shot him. Román more or less confirmed what Roberto told us."

A gust lifted the corners of Jack's *serape,* and as it rushed past Mary, the lamplight in the room flickered dramatically.

She stepped aside. "I do not want my brother to get chilled. Come inside."

Scanning the room as he went in, Jack found that they were alone. "How is he?"

"He is resting," she said coldly. Upon closing the door, Mary evidently saw Jack clearly by the light of the lamp. "Your face is healing."

The wounds inflicted by Riggs in Jack's brow and temple were still tender as he checked with his fingers.

"But you are still flushed," continued Mary. "And you have lost weight. I could not leave Roberto alone, but three times I have sent Tío Longino to your door. I worried because you did not answer."

Jack was surprised; he had slept more soundly than he had thought. But that was a discussion for later.

"Listen," he said, "I think we're all in danger. Rangers could come back looking to tie Esperanza to the raid, and when they find those shoes, that's all the excuse they'll need. They won't care that nobody but Román and Natividad has any. Everybody here is a greaser to them, and I'm worried what might happen."

"It is what I have always feared for our village. What can we do?"

"I don't know. The day after the flood, you told me the people won't leave here."

"It is their *patria chica,* the little fatherland. It is my *patria chica* too, but it is the people I care about."

"So do I." He went silent, staring down at the floor and formulating his thoughts. "We've got to convince everybody how serious this is." He looked up. "Most of them were there when the Rangers threatened to burn the church. They probably don't know that the same bunch told Father Diego they'd set the whole town on fire if he didn't keep paying. Mary, I know you're not supposed to speak of village matters to the men, but—"

"You, they will listen to. You have earned the right."

"There's what? A hundred and forty people here? Everybody needs to go across the river tomorrow and stay as long as they have to. The Rangers and Army—ranchers too, probably—look at Esperanza the way they would a den of snakes, just something to exterminate. It doesn't matter who's guilty and who's not, as long as it makes them feel like they're serving justice for what bandits did."

Jack turned at another scream of a panther. The cat was still far away, and its cry was muffled by the walls, but now the night was even more ominous.

"Wish it was already daylight." he said, facing her. "There's so much we've got to do, but rousing people out of bed's not a way to convince anybody."

"Marita?"

Through an inner doorway came Roberto's quiet summons, painfully spoken.

"May I see him?" Jack asked.

Mary wouldn't answer, so he knew that she was still upset. As she took up the kerosene lamp and stepped up into the small room, Jack followed only as far as the threshold. Under the window on the right—the same window by which the three had escaped to the roof during the flood—the muchacho lay on a grass mat.

"What is it, my brother?" she asked.

"I hear Mister Landon?" Roberto asked in English.

"He is here."

"I don't see him. Where——?"

Jack didn't know if it was good or bad that the boy had asked, but he stepped inside.

"You're looking better, Roberto," he said as he approached.

"I have just changed his bandages," said Mary.

Roberto raised up on his elbows and faced Jack. "Marita is angry with you."

It was troubling enough for Jack to be aware of the rift and let it linger unvoiced, but to hear it brought up so bluntly—and by Roberto himself—added to the pressures of the moment.

"I know," Jack said penitently, choosing not to look at Mary. "She's got good reason."

"I don't remember that night," said the muchacho.

"I was pretty rough with you. I'd come close to dying, and I wasn't myself. I'm sorry. That's something I need to say to her too. I'm hoping both of you can forgive me."

Now Jack did look at Mary, but Roberto quickly drew his attention again.

"I never forget what you say up on hill. That's why I tell Marita not be angry with you."

"Not——?"

"*Mi papá* tell me what to do," Roberto said with pride. " 'Do what's right, Roberto,' he say. 'I'm your role model, like Mister Landon say. Do what's right.' "

Now Jack did glance at Mary, and he found her looking back.

"Is that why they shot you, Roberto?" asked Jack. "You were doing what your papá would have wanted?"

"*Sí*—should say, *yes*. Papa always there, whispering. He here now, telling me to speak the English like in school."

Jack had almost forgotten. "Speaking of school, I brought you something." He displayed the papers in his hand. " 'Roberto and the Little Burro.' You never did find out what happened to the two of you."

Roberto's face lighted up in a way that Jack had never thought he would see again. Grinning as much as the bandages and pain would allow, the muchacho reached for the handwritten manuscript.

"Maybe your sister can help you read it," said Jack, relinquishing the copy.

Just scanning the title page widened Roberto's smile more. "Every night out cold and hungry, I would wonder about the little burro. It's my favorite story!"

In all Jack's years in the writing business, he had seen *Jack Bedford Landon* splashed across hundreds of editions of the *Daily Standard*. He had heard the plaudits of editors and fellow reporters and the public at large, and nine times a story bearing his byline had received accolades in direct competition with the largest newspapers in the state. Yet never before had a compliment meant so much to him, and he considered again whether *this* was the kind of writing he had been born to do.

"It is kind of Mister Landon to bring it," said Mary.

There was forgiveness in her tone, and in her eyes as well when Jack turned to her. Still, there was so much the two of them needed to discuss, but another cry of a panther focused Jack's attention.

"Roberto, would you be able stir around tomorrow?"

"He has been much stronger today," said Mary.

"We're going to have to leave here," Jack continued. "Everbody in Esperanza's going to have to go. After what happened at Christmas, the authorities will be here, and it'll be an eye for an eye and a tooth for a tooth." He gave Mary a quick look. "Isn't that how your father's Bible puts it? We can't let them catch any of us here."

"But Papa's grave is here!" contended Roberto.

"Our mother's too," Mary added quietly.

"And the cross he make!" the boy went on. Then a terrible sadness masked his face. "Is it my fault, Marita? Everybody leaving—my fault?"

When Mary seemed not to know what to say, Jack spoke up. "Was the raid your idea, Roberto? You the one leading it? They all do what a fifteen year old tells them?"

Sometimes, helping a person discover his own answers was the most powerful of arguments, and it seemed that way with Roberto.

"I hate them!" the boy exclaimed. "They kill Mexicanos same as gringos—good Mexicanos, good gringos. They kill to take what they want. Papa say, 'Stop them, Roberto! Stop them!' "

"And they shot you when you tried," completed Jack. He bent close and put a hand—a *gentle* hand this time—on the muchacho's shoulder. "You did your father proud, Roberto."

The boy's chin began to quiver, and then Jack felt a hand on his own shoulder and he turned to find Mary pressing close and looking at him, her eyes welling. For a moment, the touch of one to another connected Jack to the two most important people in his life, and the feeling didn't go away even as Roberto lay back out of reach.

This was Jack's *family*, and it was so much more than anything Annie and her white house with the picket fence could have offered.

Dogs began to bark.

From throughout the village, they barked in a way Jack had never heard before, an alarming cacophony that brought him bolt upright and facing the closed shutter.

"Jack Landon . . . ?"

There was concern in Mary's voice as her fingers tightened on Jack's arm, and when he turned, he found her lower lip pushed up in distress.

"The revolver he rode in with," said Jack. "What happened to it?"

She nodded to the doorway. "It is on the shelf over the table."

"*¡Santa Maria!*" exclaimed Roberto. "The dogs!"

"Might just be a lion," said Jack. "Roberto, if something happens, I want you to pull the cover over you and not move. Mary, soon as I get the six-shooter, blow the lamp out."

Hurrying into the other room, Jack reached for the shelf. Just as his fingers closed on the Bisley, the outside door burst open behind him with a rush of cold air. Whirling, he faced shadowy forms in the threshold, and then the lamp went out and he could no longer see.

From the door roared a six-shooter.

The ricochet whizzed through the dark, and a voice cried out over the ringing in Jack's ears.

"Put the damned gun down!"

"All right! It's on the table!" said Jack.

A light flared outside and a flaming torch swept across the doorway and came inside, playing in a *cinco peso* badge and in two sets of eyes showing above concealing bandanas.

"What is this?" Jack challenged. "You have no right—"

Rough hands seized him.

"Take him out of here!" the ranger commanded.

Dragged out into the night, Jack was helpless to do anything but look back as the torch brightened the cracks in first one thatch shutter and then another.

"Leave my home at once!"

Mary's defiant cry pierced the gloom, and Jack fought against the restraining hands.

"Don't touch her!" he shouted into the house. "You hear me? Leave her alone!"

But the fiery cracks in the bedroom shutter dimmed and seethed as figures evidently moved against the torch inside.

"My brother is sick!" Jack heard Mary exclaim. "He must stay in bed!"

"What you got under them bandages, pepper belly?" demanded a gravelly voice.

There came a sharp cry of pain.

"Sick, hell!" added the voice. "Been shot, ain't ya. You'll pay more than that for what you done at Brite's."

Jack continued to resist and yell toward the house as swearing men forced him into the street and leftward toward the mission. Ahead, the plaza swarmed with ghostly figures that protested in two languages, while on either side of Jack more torches swept through the adobes and pushed increasing numbers of frightened villagers into the street.

"Find ever' gun!" a voice instructed.

Jack could see only so much by moonlight, but he estimated the raiders to number forty, far more than Ranger Company B's full force of eleven regulars. The few ranchers typically sworn as Special Rangers could have constituted only part of the remainder, making it clear that many of the men had no legal authority—hence the need to hide behind masks. But one and all were cruel, striking uncooperative hombres and manhandling the señoras. There was no consideration of rights or due process, for in their eyes the people of Esperanza were inferiors. Even if they weren't bandits or collaborators, they were greasers, tools with which to strike fear in every Mexican along the border and deter another raid.

Mary's welfare concerned Jack above all else, and when he called out to her multiple times without a response, he panicked. *The bastards! If they touched her . . . !* Then out of the bedlam came an answering "Jack Landon! Jack Landon!"—a momentary reprieve in a desperate hour.

A fire blazed in the nearing plaza, the flames leaping at the night, and silhouettes descended on it from all directions. It was now bitterly cold, exacerbated by a moaning wind that threatened to peel the hide from Jack's face. Numbed to the bone, he didn't even have his *serape* to draw around him, not since an assailant had stripped him of it. The looming fire promised warmth; at what price, Jack had no idea. But for now he could only imagine the suffering of Mary and Roberto—*Roberto*, the pitiful boy whose anguish already would have tested the strongest of men.

As if they were cattle, Jack and the other villagers were herded into the plaza, where shivering hombres and señoras, with their confused children, already huddled around the popping fire. Through the bitter, swirling smoke, Jack could see his students and Father Diego and Tío Longino, the firelight burning in their worried eyes. But the tossing flames also captured the tight mouth, flaring nostrils, and cocked head of a man who wore the *cinco peso*, and as soon as Jack recognized the sergeant, he shouted at him.

"Wolfe with an *E*! These are American citizens!"

Wolfe spun, and the way the fire raged in his eyes made him seem like something out of perdition. Maybe on this night he was.

"You're outside your rights!" Jack added.

"Like hell!" Wolfe turned to a masked man. "Drag those SOBs up here!"

Clutched by Ranger accomplices, two figures squirmed in the crowd, and in moments Román and Natividad emerged just as Jack expected—with the bonfire alive in their shiny new foot-wear.

"Hamilton-Brown shoes, right out of Brite's Store!" said Wolfe.

Restrained, Román and Natividad kept their gazes down, but Wolfe grabbed the older brother by the hair and yanked his head up.

"Look at me! What kind of devil hangs a man upside down from a rafter and cuts his throat?" Then Wolfe similarly forced Natividad to face him. "Shoot two men dead and scare the hell out of women and girls on Christmas Day—you damned greasers! I ought to cut your throats the same way!"

The raid on Brite Ranch had been more heinous than Jack had thought. These men were out for blood, wherever they might find it, and he was suddenly terrified of where this was headed.

"Two pair of shoes don't convict a whole town!" he argued.

Wolfe turned his glare on Jack. "I answer to Captain Fox, not to you. What's it take for you to learn your lesson about causing trouble?"

"There's a hundred and forty people here, and you've got two pair of shoes. That's not evidence!"

But more and more villagers continued to crowd the fire, until surely there could have been none left in their homes. Surrounded by armed men, all they could do was cower and shiver as the rangers prevented the free movement that might have allowed the outermost a better share of the warm flames. By voice Jack identified Mary's location and learned that her brother was with her, but the throng and the heavy shadows denied him even a glimpse.

Weapons began to collect at Wolfe's feet as men returned from a sweep of the homes, and when a ranger straggled in with a few skinning knives and reported, "That's the last of 'em," Jack counted the firearms glinting in the firelight.

Two shotguns.

Two rifles.

And three revolvers, including the Bisley.

"That's all?" Jack challenged. "Seven firearms in all of Esperanza? What kind of armory is that for a whole village of bandits, Wolfe?"

The ranger sergeant didn't answer, and Jack's voice quietened.

"Let the people go back to their homes," he pleaded, his tone no longer confrontational. "They're cold and tired and you're scaring everybody. These people aren't a threat. Let them go back."

But Wolfe had other ideas.

"Take the men off by themselves!" he ordered.

Fearing the worst, women and children began to scream and beg for the lives of the men. It was heartbreaking, and it was made all the worse by Mary's cries. But Jack had his own concerns as ranger accomplices dragged him past the fire and threw him up against the mission's courtyard wall. There, forced into a lineup with the other men, he shivered to the chilling wind that shrieked through the graveyard at his back like something fiendish.

From right to left, Wolfe and a torch-bearing ranger started down the row toward him in inspection. The anticipation and uncertainty were torture, and Jack grew weak in the knees as Wolfe began to select villagers one by one.

This one.

Him.

That pepper belly there.

Upon Wolfe's directive, rangers escorted the selected men off to the side, and Jack didn't know who had more reason to fear: the chosen or those who remained. Then Wolfe growled, "These two, for damned sure," and when rangers pulled Román and Natividad out of the lineup, Jack at least knew which group was under the greater threat.

Suddenly a dangling bandage, stained with blood, showed in the torch light, and when heartless hands took a wobbling Roberto away, Jack cried out and tried to break free.

"Leave him alone! He's just a boy!"

A guard was suddenly in Jack's face, a crosswise carbine driving hard into his chest and forcing him back. But Jack continued to shout.

"Don't do this, Wolfe! He's fifteen! Please don't do this!"

Wolfe didn't acknowledge Jack with even a glance, and a moment later rough hands also took Tío Longino Castaneda away.

"He's an old man!" yelled Jack. "The boy's fifteen and he's seventy-two! They're not threats to anybody!"

Jack continued to plead until Wolfe stopped before him, and there was nothing in the ranger sergeant's fire-burnished features to suggest mercy.

"You taking us out to shoot us?" Jack demanded, knowing he would be next. "That what you're doing?"

"You and your damned letter to the governor," snapped Wolfe. "Wouldn't stop me for a minute if I thought you had something to do with Brite's. You's damned lucky I know the condition you was in the day before."

Wolfe moved on down the line, and Jack continued to petition for the lives of Mary's brother and the caring man she had always called Tío, Uncle. Meanwhile, from among those Wolfe had passed by, came Father Diego's quavering voice.

"Esperanza's day of reckoning has come. Now we must hold to hope."

CHAPTER 24

It's all right, mi hijo, my son.

Roberto's father seemed to whisper in the wind as armed men led the boy away in the freezing dark with fourteen other villagers to the pleas and wails of the women and children. Marita's cries were among them, and Roberto could also hear Jack Landon's desperate appeal.

"Please reconsider! I'm begging you, Wolfe! He's just a boy. An old man. You've got the fathers of forty or fifty children!"

But the rangers stayed silent as the bonfire receded and the way ahead waited in the gloom. At gunpoint they prodded Roberto and the others around the courtyard's left corner and past the mission's west face, and the march continued until sentinel hill loomed up on the right. Always before, the bluff had seemed a guarding presence, but tonight it was like something out of hell perched black against the moonlit sky.

The rangers turned the foremost prisoners up the steep slope, and as Roberto weakly followed in their wake, he stumbled and would have fallen if not for Longino Castaneda's quick hand on his arm.

"I've got you, little muchacho," said the huffing *viejo.*

Roberto regained his balance, but every step higher was a struggle even with assistance.

"Why you, Tío?" he asked in Spanish. "The ones they took . . . Why you?"

"Where God wills, even the saints can do nothing. Maybe He

chose old Longino to help the little brother of my Mariposita. *Sí*, to help you the same way the blessed Simon carried the cross of Jesucristo."

"I carried the cross *mi papá* made," Roberto said proudly. "Up this hill, I helped him when I was young."

"Ah, your papá." Suddenly Tío grew emotional. "Our Lady has honored me to spend my last walk with the son of my *amigo*—my *amigo* from boyhood."

"Your last walk, Tío?"

Through Tío Longino's grip on his arm, Roberto felt a shudder, and for a moment the old man couldn't speak.

"God's will is to be done." He looked at Roberto in the moonlight, and his voice began to tremble. "These are very bad men."

Roberto knew it. They were as evil as the bandits of Chico Cano, but Roberto took comfort in what lay at the hill's summit.

"I'm not afraid, Tío. From the cross, Papa will watch over me."

"*Sí*, little muchacho, and so will Jesucristo. Whatever is to happen, He will be with us."

At the pumping legs of the prisoner in front of him, Roberto broke over the summit with Tío Longino to find, near the bluff's point, the arm of the cross blazed against the full moon. The cross stood so straight and sturdy, a kingly silhouette outlined by moon glow along its edge. Roberto had never seen anything so beautiful; it was worthy of not only his father, but of Jesucristo Himself, and the boy felt blessed to have done his part in making sure it continued to watch over Esperanza, the village whose name meant hope.

The armed men took Roberto and the other prisoners along the mesa a short distance to the left, away from the cross and out of the sight of the villagers in the plaza. In the ensuing lineup, Roberto realized that Román and his brother were at his right shoulder.

"Why did they bring us here, Román?" asked Natividad. "Why did—"

"Don't be a fool," said Román. "They're going to kill us."

"No, Román, no! They'll ask questions and let us go back!"

There was a sharp pop, and Roberto knew that Román had cuffed his brother on the ear.

"You had to have shoes, *pendejo*," accused Román. "It's your fault!"

"You took shoes first, Román. When I went in the store, you had them in your hands!"

From the unforgiving army of dark figures who faced them out of a sky that burned with the swollen moon, the voice of the commanding ranger was unmistakable.

"Don't matter much now, does it. Him grabbing Hamilton-Browns first or you doing it."

Then the ranger's voice rose and seemed to shake the ground under Roberto's feet. "Turn around, all you murdering greasers!"

Roberto did as he was told. He would have liked to look upon the cross to the very end, but when he closed his eyes he learned that he could still see it. *Sí*, it was as beautiful as ever, a fitting image to accompany Tío Longino's whispers from alongside for the Mother of God to pray for them in this hour of their deaths.

From behind came the click-click of carbines readying to fire, and in the wind Roberto heard his father's voice a final time.

Come to me, mi hijo.

The volley from sentinel hill pierced the night as if hell itself had ruptured.

As distraught as the villagers in the plaza had been before, utter hysteria gripped them now. The outcry and wails around Jack were indescribable, and as wives and sons and daughters broke with other townspeople for the guards who held them back from the bluff, he feared the first gunshot that could precipitate a massacre of all of Esperanza.

Mary was as terror-stricken as any of them, for Jack glimpsed her bolting with the pell-mell rush. He shouldered his way through and seized her, only to feel her fists on his chest as she tried to wrench free.

"It's me!"

He didn't know if she heard him as he pulled her down to the greater safety of the ground. He held her there, shielding and saying her name until she recognized him, while all around them the firelight flashed against feet and legs that milled like devils dancing in perdition.

"My brother!" she said.

"There's nothing we can do. Stay down—they could shoot!"

Somehow the guards quelled the panicked flight without firing a shot, but there was nothing that could calm a people who wept and moaned in anguish. Jack trembled with Mary where they lay, his dread almost more than he could endure. Suddenly the screams resumed, and he rose with her and understood why.

From out of the shadows toward sentinel hill came figures, and as they rounded the corner of the courtyard wall, they took shape:

Wolfe and ten men, their carbines twinkling in the light of the bonfire like stars that never hinted of gloom.

Wolfe and ten men, and not a single villager they had dragged away into the night.

"What have you done, Wolfe?" Jack cried. "You son of a bitch, what have you done?"

But the sergeant ignored him, and soon riders brought up a

sizable remuda, the horses already saddled. With the rangers and their accomplices preoccupied with finding their respective mounts, they no longer picketed the courtyard wall, and Jack knew what he had to do.

Placing his hands on Mary's shoulders, he saw the emotion on her cheeks glistening in the firelight, and he felt for her.

"Don't go up there!" he pleaded quietly.

Bending low, he slipped through the throng and came out near Father Diego. Only here, near the courtyard gate, would Jack be exposed, but when he whispered, "Try to keep the families away," the old padre seemed to understand. A few strategic steps in concert with Father Diego in his wind-swelled vestments allowed Jack to slink unseen through the arch.

Respecting the graves in contrast to the desecration by Riggs, he crept northwest across the courtyard and went over the wall where it connected to the mission's west side. The way was clear now, except for a dark veil that seemed to cover sentinel hill. Jack was afraid to pass through it, afraid because he knew what he would see, afraid because of what it would mean not only to him but to Mary and all of Esperanza.

Summoning his courage as he gained the base of the west slope, Jack was startled by the thunder of hoofs. Looking back, he saw the rangers and their cohorts riding away toward the river, and they celebrated with yells like the Comanche war whoops that an old Indian fighter had once described to Jack.

Damn them to hell!

With a fury unlike anything he had known before, Jack stormed the slope and burst over the rim. The first thing he saw was the cross at two o'clock, and it had a strange beauty, backlit as it was by the moon so that a thin glow along its edge traced it perfectly against the sky. The writer Jack had been would have described its appearance as ethereal, even mesmerizing. Indeed, its soft luminescence captivated him in a way he couldn't understand and somehow muted the rage that moments ago had been beyond restraint.

Looking left, he saw the forms on the ground, a row laid out almost neatly so that it partially dissected the mesa. Jack approached reverently, struck by the play of moonlight on the bodies as if they lay in state under a celestial votive candle. One form, in particular, stretched out two-thirds of the way down the line, drew him closer, for about the head a shining band of white presented an almost halo effect.

At Roberto's feet, Jack stopped and stared, oblivious for a moment to the wind's brutal cold and everything else but a prostrate boy who had tried to make things right and had died for it. Close by on Roberto's right lay Tío Longino Castaneda, his white whiskers unmistakable as he faced the boy he had affectionately called "little muchacho." Touchingly, the old man's hand rested on Roberto's shoulder, as if at the last breath he had sought to comfort the young son of the man who had been his *compadre* since boyhood.

Kneeling, Jack gently removed the *viejo's* hand and rolled the boy on his back. The open eyes were blank as they reflected moonlight—confirmation, if Jack needed any, that Roberto was dead. Taking him in his arms, not caring that the clothes were wet with blood, Jack held him close in shock and disbelief and then stood, the loose bandage streaming in the wind as the head fell back.

Jack turned, unaccountably drawn to the cross, and went to it with burdens greater than he could bear. Laying the body across the base, he looked up and studied the radiance of the vertical shaft and the extended arms, beams that represented a cross from another time and place, one that suddenly seemed to speak to him with a still, small voice.

Sinking to his knees, a man stripped of the pride and ego that had considered religion a crutch, a man whose intellect confirmed so much and yet failed to understand far more, Jack chose to believe. Here on a lonely hill that overlooked a far-flung village that he had come to love—a hill now stained by the blood of innocents—Jack *chose* to believe and accept the peace that came with it. His long, dark search down the road to nowhere was over, for at the end of nowhere lay Hope.

Ever since the two of them had prepared Roberto's body for burial and laid it in repose under the window in the boy's room, Jack had knelt with Mary in prayer before the remains as the sound of bitter weeping had hung over the village. The whispering votive candles on the sill had flickered for half the night now, and Jack could wait no longer.

"Mary, there's something I need to tell you," he said quietly.

"Yes?"

He stood and drew her away from so solemn a place. She was pale and dry-eyed, a person drained of all feeling, and Jack wondered if she would even grasp what he was about to tell her.

"I've got to go away for a while," he said.

"You are leaving?" she asked incredulously.

Jack wasn't sure if the sudden life in her voice was for the better.

"I'd never go off at a time like this—not when you're grieving so, not when I'm grieving with you. But this can't wait, not even till morning. I've already talked to Father Diego, and he's going to make sure you're taken care of."

"You are leaving?" she asked again, and this time her deadened emotions welled up in her eyes.

"I'd rather not even say why. It's a shot in the dark—I doubt it will do any good—so I don't even want to get my hopes up, much less yours."

"You will . . . You will come back?" In her voice was a degree of fear he had never heard before.

"Listen, Mary. Something happened to me up on that hill tonight. The things you told me about a cross, the bits and pieces I picked up from Father Diego, the things I read in your father's Bible—it all became real to me. There's a clarity and an acceptance that was never there before. I guess that's what faith is. So when I tell you I'll be back, God willing, I say it as someone who believes that a lie won't go unpunished."

"You promise you will come back?" she pressed.

"I mean it just as much as when I told you I love you." He stroked her hair where it fell across her cheek. "Whether you can ever say the same to me doesn't make any difference. I promise I'll be back, because this village named Hope is my home, and it needs my help more than ever now."

"You know that I love you, Jack Landon!"

"Then I want to leave you with a question to think about while I'm gone. Work through your grief first, the best you can. I know it's going to be hard on you. You lost your brother and Tío and a lot of others. But when I come back, I hope you can give me an answer."

"Yes, Jack Landon?"

"I want to know if you'll marry me."

CHAPTER 25

Jack thought he had put behind him forever the dusty boardwalk fronting even dustier Chadbourne Street, but as he stepped up, it sagged and creaked familiarly under his dressy, white-and-black boots.

The tinkling of a piano from the nearby Wylie Hardware Company Saloon was also the same, and the syncopated strains followed him to the door of the modest frame building still crushed between two-story brick structures. Once there, Jack took a moment to collect himself and straighten the gray-wool summer suit that was badly in need of pressing.

He was returning to the *San Angelo Daily Standard* in the same way he had left it, except that now he was a different person. He had written the pages in his hand for the right reasons, not for the fleeting gratification of someone's praise or a citation of achievement. Over long, cold miles on a borrowed horse, and later on a Kansas City, Mexico and Orient train, he had crafted and re-crafted the pages, and finally he was at the culmination of a mission.

He went in, and he was glad that deadline was approaching because it spared him the stunned looks of the reporters and copyeditor who were busy fighting the clock. Besides, when Jack turned left down a hall and followed the cigar smoke inside a left-side office, the jaw of the short, stocky man went slack enough as he looked up from behind a cluttered desk.

"You probably don't want to see me, and I'm not here to ask

for my job back," said Jack. "But I've got something I think you'll be interesting in running."

"You're thinner than I remember," said his former editor.

"I've been through some things," said Jack. Then he added his own observation. "You've got less hair."

The editor cracked a smile and ran a hand over his bald pate, and it seemed to relax the tension.

"I lost what little I had when the best reporter in the state disappeared on me. Where have you been?"

Jack extended the pages. "This will answer a lot."

His onetime mentor laid his cigar aside and accepted the rumpled manuscript.

"Handwritten?" he remarked.

"Not many typewriters where I was. You have time to read it? I'll wait in the lobby."

"Coffee's fresh. Give me a few minutes. It'll take a while to figure out this hen-scratching."

"Not easy to write from the hurricane deck of a horse."

The editor drew back a little in surprise. "You always were one for creativity," he said. "Jack, it's good to see you."

In the lobby, Jack poured himself coffee and sat down with a gratis copy of the Sunday paper. To the clack-clack of typewriters in the newsroom, he thumbed through, smelling the newsprint as the pages rustled. In the society section, a story midway down the third column caught his eye:

Watson-Peterson Nuptials

Mr. and Mrs. L. Watson of Tom Green County announce the marriage of their daughter, Annie Watson, to A. D. Peterson at their home on Christmas Eve.

Jack read no farther. Annie Watson. *His* Annie. On Christmas

Eve, Jack had struggled to survive in and out of the rock hellhole at the old mining claim. Nevertheless, he was genuinely happy that Annie had moved on with her life so quickly. He just hoped that she would now have the trim, white house with the picket fence of her dreams.

With one loose end cleared up, Jack would pay his father a visit before starting back for Esperanza. With Jack's newfound faith had come a capacity for forgiveness, even for a man who wanted to deny him a life of his own choosing and who unjustly blamed him for his mother's death.

"Jack."

Deep in reverie, Jack had lost track of time. Turning, he found the editor puffing away on a fresh cigar as he approached from the hall, the worn pages in his hand. Jack rose as the older man came up before him, and Jack didn't know what to think when the editor thumped the pages and gave a quick wag of his head. But one word from him said it all.

"Sensational."

"It works?" asked Jack.

"It's a hell of a story. I've never read anything like it, not even from you. With the credibility the Jack Bedford Landon byline has earned, this is going to blow the lid off things in Austin. Every paper in the country will run it. Fifteen men and boys executed without due process. My God, what a nightmare."

"You think it will change anything?"

"I've learned you can't predict politicians or state agencies. But if this story doesn't kick-start change, nothing will. I tell you, Jack, this is the kind of frontline reporting that journalism is all about. What time is it? Write it down—this is going to get you the Pulitzer Prize."

"Do me a favor, will you?" asked Jack. "Don't enter it."

"Hell, son, why not?"

"I found a prize on a hilltop, and I don't need another one."

"I don't know what that means," said the editor, "but I'll bet you, once you're back in the saddle at your old desk, I can talk you into it. I'm talking a *Pulitzer*, Jack."

Jack shook his head. "I appreciate the job offer, but I've written my last news story."

"I hope you'll reconsider. You'll be wasting the best talent I've ever seen. What else will you do with your life?"

Jack thought of a far-off village, its people hurting and in need, and a dark-haired señorita whom he prayed would give him the answer he wanted.

"I hope," he said, "I still have a story to finish living."

They had more to say to each other, but it wasn't until Jack started to leave that the editor told him about his father.

"You do know that he died two weeks ago? The lawyer handling his estate came in last week, looking for you. The way he talked, you're sole heir to a substantial estate. His name's Smithson, and his office is across the street."

Jack found Mary in the courtyard, a forlorn figure kneeling among the fresh graves.

It was early morning in Esperanza, and as he approached from behind, his long shadow showed the way between the newly set crosses. A breeze stirred the recently turned dirt, and over its murmur he could hear her whispering. At first, he thought she prayed, but when he neared and could look over her shoulder, he saw that she read from papers too white in the sun to distinguish. Stopping, he listened.

"Placing the rope around the orphaned animal, Roberto began leading it back down the rain-swept arroyo. But the little burro had ideas of its own, and it bolted in the opposite direction. Caught by surprise, the boy was facedown in the muck before he knew it, his hand still fast on the rope.

"Roberto didn't have any quit in him, but neither did the

burro. Its small hoofs churning, the animal was away to the races, dragging the tumbling boy through slime so disgusting that he figured he would be spitting mud for a month."

Pausing, she gave an almost inaudible laugh, bittersweet in its pathos, and brushed her cheek.

"Mary," said Jack, "I'm home."

She twisted about, wide-eyed and with a little gasp, and burst to her feet. "Are you really here, Jack Landon? Tell me it is not another dream!"

"If I'm with you, it's a dream I don't want to wake up from."

She came into his arms, and he could feel her trembling from so many crippling emotions.

"I was gone longer than I thought I'd be," he said when she eventually withdrew. "I'm sorry."

"I listened to your promise. I knew that you would come back after you helped our village."

"I never told you why I was leaving," Jack said in surprise.

"You did not have to. I always knew that you had a servant's heart, thanks be to God."

"You must have seen a promise of something in me that I'm still not sure myself is there. But you're right about me going off to help Esperanza, and all the Esperanzas like it. I probably won't know if I did any good for months, if ever. But there was something I didn't expect that's going to make a difference when the first freight wagon gets here next week."

"Oh?"

Jack glanced up at sentinel hill's cross, just visible past the mission bell tower. "How many children were left without fathers up there that night?"

Mary, too, looked up at sentinel hill for a moment, and she made the sign of the cross before answering.

"Father Diego has blessed forty-two little ones."

"It's a loss they'll suffer from for the rest of their lives. But at least I have the means now to make sure they'll have what they need and not ever go hungry. The same goes for the whole village."

"How can that be?" she asked.

"I found out my father died. Everything he had is mine now."

Now it was Mary who grieved with Jack, and the pain showed in her face and then in her lingering embrace.

"I am sorry, Jack Landon. I am sorry!"

When they stood apart again, Jack drew upon the assurance that faith had brought.

" 'Where God wills, even the saints are powerless,' " he quoted. "Isn't that what the people say? I guess this is His way of taking care of Esperanza."

The pages in Mary's hand rustled in a sudden gust, drawing Jack's attention.

" 'Roberto and the Little Burro'?" he asked.

"My brother never had a chance to read the rest of your story. Only Jesucristo knows if he can hear, but I am closer to Roberto when I read at his grave."

They fell silent, and as they looked at one another, the question that Jack had left for Mary to consider and pray about became a powerful presence, even as it persisted unspoken. As he searched her eyes, he couldn't tell if she waited for him to ask it again, or dreaded its mention. Finally she broke the lull.

"God will bless your pledge to the children of Esperanza. Now there is another promise for you to make, Jack Landon."

"Anything."

She checked the pages in her hand and smiled at him in a new and special way.

"Promise me," she whispered, "that you will write a story for each of our own children."

EPILOGUE

JUNE 4, 1918—Despite attempts by Texas Rangers Company B and others to cover up or justify their role in the killings, Governor William P. Hobby disbands Company B and fires several of its rangers for "shooting men upon no provocation when they were helpless and disarmed." He also takes action against J. M. Fox, captain of Company B:

Austin, Texas, July 3, 1918
Capt. J. M. Fox
Marfa, Texas
Dear Sir:
   . . . Fifteen Mexicans were killed while in the custody of your men after they had been arrested and disarmed. This is verified by all proof . . .

The trouble maker and lawless Ranger has no place on the border . . . All peace officers should know that every man whether he is white or black, yellow or brown, has the constitutional right to a trial by jury, and that no organized band operating under the laws of this State has the right to constitute itself judge and jury, and executioner . . .

Your forced resignation came in the interest of humanity, decency, law and order, and I submit that now and hereafter the laws of the Constitution of this State must be superior to the autocratic will of any peace officer.

Very truly yours,

(Signed) Jas. A. Harley

Brigadier General—The Adjutant General, State of Texas

AUTHOR'S NOTE

This novel is based in part on the events surrounding the unauthorized execution of fifteen unarmed men and boys of Mexican heritage at Porvenir, Texas, by Texas Rangers and their accomplices on January 28, 1918, in retaliation for the Brite Ranch raid south of Valentine, Texas, on Christmas Day in 1917. Of note, no solid evidence tied any of the executed individuals to the raid, and no one involved in the mass execution was ever indicted.

My most important sources were:

"Adjutant General to Capt. Fox," *The New Era* (Marfa, Texas), July 27, 1918. This is the letter, excerpted in the epilogue and dated July 3, 1918, from Adjutant General James A. Harley to Captain J. M. Fox.

"Proceedings of the Joint Committee of the Senate and the House in the Investigation of the Texas State Ranger Force" (convened in Austin, Texas, January 31, 1919), continuation of charges brought by J. T. Canales, 77th District Representative, 144–48; testimony of C. B. Hudspeth, 966–67; and "In Re of the Investigation of the El Porvenir Fight of January 28, 1918 in Presidio County, Texas" (eyewitness and hearsay statements regarding the events at Porvenir), 1,586–1,605; Texas State Library and Archives Commission, Austin, Texas.

"Shooting of Fifteen Mexicans Blamed of Raiding Starts Quiz," *Bismarck Evening Tribune*, February 8, 1918.

Warren, Harry, "The Porvenir Massace [sic] in Presidio County,

219

Texas On January 28, 1918," manuscript, Harry Warren Papers 1835–1932, Archives of the Big Bend, Sul Ross State University, Alpine, Texas. Warren was a schoolteacher in Porvenir during the events.

Warren, Harry, "Porvenir Massacre," manuscript with lists of victims and participating Texas Rangers and accomplices, Clifford B. Casey Papers 1882–1981, Archives of the Big Bend.

I also consulted:

Justice, Glenn, *Little Known History of the Texas Big Bend* (Odessa, TX: Rimrock Press, 2001), 148–58.

Miles, Elton, *More Tales of the Big Bend* (College Station: Texas A&M University Press, 1988), 158–63.

ABOUT THE AUTHOR

Similar to the main character in this novel, **Patrick Dearen** received nine state and national awards as a young reporter for the *San Angelo Standard-Times* and another West Texas newspaper. He is now the author of twenty-six books. His ten nonfiction works include *A Cowboy of the Pecos; Castle Gap and the Pecos Frontier, Revisited;* and *The Last of the Old-Time Cowboys.* His research has led to sixteen novels, including *The Big Drift*, winner of the Spur Award of Western Writers of America. His other novels include *When Cowboys Die* (a Spur Award finalist), *Perseverance, When the Sky Rained Dust, The Illegal Man, To Hell or the Pecos, Dead Man's Boot, Apache Lament,* and *Haunted Border.*

A wilderness enthusiast and ragtime pianist, Dearen lives with his wife, Mary, in Texas. Visit patrickdearen.com for more information.

The employees of Five Star Publishing hope you have enjoyed this book.

Our Five Star novels explore little-known chapters from America's history, stories told from unique perspectives that will entertain a broad range of readers.

Other Five Star books are available at your local library, bookstore, all major book distributors, and directly from Five Star/Gale.

Connect with Five Star Publishing

Website:
  gale.com/five-star

Facebook:
  facebook.com/FiveStarCengage

Twitter:
  twitter.com/FiveStarCengage

Email:
  FiveStar@cengage.com

For information about titles and placing orders:
  (800) 223-1244
  gale.orders@cengage.com

To share your comments, write to us:
  Five Star Publishing
  Attn: Publisher
  10 Water St., Suite 310
  Waterville, ME 04901